Cade's jaw clenc...
"You could have...

"But I wasn't," Mariah said stubbornly. "And you wouldn't be yelling if this had happened to anyone else on the crew."

His eyes flared with heat and before Mariah could blink, he wrapped his arms around her, hauled her up against his hard body and took her mouth with his.

The kiss wasn't sweet, nor cajoling, nor slowly sensual. It was purely carnal and reeked of domination and desperation.

Mariah reeled under the instant surge of heat that flooded her, but she fought the need to give in to the desire to meet lust with lust and struggled to get her hands between them to push at his chest. He was immovable.

Dear Reader,

Like many little girls, I adored horses and cowboys, but I truly fell in love with Montana at the age of five when my family moved onto my great-uncle's homestead in Butte Creek. I've been fascinated by the American West ever since and I was so pleased when Silhouette agreed to let me write another miniseries set in Montana. This first story in the Big Sky Brothers belongs to Cade Coulter—eldest of four sons born to Joseph Coulter. When Joseph dies, Cade is the first to come home to the Triple C Ranch in Indian Springs, Montana, where the brothers grew up. Cade and his brothers must find a way to pay inheritance taxes or they'll lose the ranch that's been in their family for generations.

Fortunately Cade has allies—one of whom is beautiful Mariah Jones. Though he questions her motives, he can't ignore the passion between them.

I hope you enjoy Cade's story and that you'll join me soon for the story of the second brother to return to Montana—Zach Coulter, who brings his special brand of expertise to aid in the struggle to save the huge Triple C Ranch he loves.

Warmly,

~Lois

CADE COULTER'S RETURN

LOIS FAYE DYER

Silhouette

SPECIAL EDITION

Published by Silhouette Books

America's Publisher of Contemporary Romance

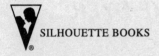

SILHOUETTE BOOKS

Recycling programs for this product may not exist in your area.

ISBN-13: 978-0-373-65556-4

CADE COULTER'S RETURN

Copyright © 2010 by Lois Faye Dyer

Visit Silhouette Books at www.eHarlequin.com

Printed in U.S.A.

LOIS FAYE DYER

lives in a small town on the shore of beautiful Puget Sound in the Pacific Northwest with her two eccentric and lovable cats, Chloe and Evie. She loves to hear from readers. You can write to her c/o Paperbacks Plus, 1618 Bay Street, Port Orchard, WA 98366. Visit her on the Web at www.LoisDyer.com.

With thanks to my brother's good friends—
Randy and Cathy Brisbane, Denise Johnson,
Mike and Sherie Brisbane, Arline Vanoli and Crist Bass.
Your kindness is deeply appreciated.

Prologue

Cade Coulter leaned against the fender of his old pickup truck, arms crossed over his chest as he stared at the closed door of the Triple C ranch house. His younger brother Zach was still inside.

What the hell is taking him so long? Cade glanced impatiently at his wristwatch. *It's seven o'clock.*

The June sunshine was already warm on his face. He slipped aviator sunglasses on his nose, turning his head to sweep the ranch yard with a swift, assessing glance. The Triple C was the biggest ranch in northeast Montana. He'd been born and raised here and every day of his twenty-two years had been spent riding over the Coulter Cattle Company's vast acres, working cattle under the hot sun of summer and the cold wind of winter snows.

But he and his three brothers had made a pact—they'd

all sworn to stay on the ranch only until the youngest, Eli, had graduated from high school. And last night, Eli had walked across the stage to collect his diploma. This morning, Cade was leaving the Triple C and Montana for good. He doubted he'd ever be back. He swept a longer, slower glance over the buildings clustered around a central graveled yard. He'd helped paint the big barn, house, bunkhouse and assorted outbuildings more times than he could count.

His gaze reached the grove of trees beyond the barn and halted. Hidden behind the green leaves and sturdy trunks was his mother's shuttered studio and the creek that flowed past it.

A sharp stab of grief edged with guilt sliced through him. But with the stoicism and relentless control gained over the ten years since his mother's death, he instantly sealed the emotions away. He'd learned long ago that regrets were useless.

"Cade."

He turned to see his two youngest brothers, Brodie and Eli, loping down the steps of the bunkhouse before striding toward him across the ranch yard.

"You two ready to go?" he asked as they neared, noting the duffel bags each had slung over their shoulders.

"Yeah." Eli's green gaze flicked over the four pickups parked in front of the house. "Where's Zach?"

"He's still inside." Cade saw the swift frown that creased Eli's brow.

"Let's go get him." Brodie's voice was curt.

Eli nodded and walked through the open gate to the house yard, up the curved sidewalk to the porch.

Cade and Brodie followed him.

"Was Dad drinking when you got in last night?" Cade asked.

"Don't know," Brodie replied. "I didn't get home till after two this morning and I slept in the bunkhouse." He nodded at Eli's broad back ahead of them. "So did Eli."

They jogged up the steps, joining Eli as he opened the door. All three of them stepped over the threshold, Cade first, just as Zach, the oldest of his three younger brothers, came down the stairs, a bulging duffel bag in one hand.

Their father stood across the wide living room next to the fireplace, his big frame rigid. His flushed face was proof enough for Cade that Joseph Coulter had either started drinking whiskey when he left his bed or that he was still drunk from the night before.

"If you leave, don't come back—not until you get a letter from my lawyer telling you I'm dead."

The bitter, harsh words rang in the quiet room. Zach halted on the stairs. Beside him, Cade felt Eli and Brodie tense and go still. Cade's gaze never left his father and he didn't flinch under Joseph's fierce stare. For a long moment, his father's hate and accusation raged between them, though neither spoke. Then Joseph's gaze flicked past Cade to Brodie.

Cade's fingers curled into fists but he didn't comment. He looked at Zach, gave a slight nod, and turned on this heel to leave the house. He heard his brothers' boots echo on the porch boards behind him as he strode down the sidewalk and reached his truck, yanking the door open. His muscles were tight with the effort to keep his anger under control, but on some level he was glad to feel its burn. If he focused on the anger, he didn't have to think about the wrenching pain of leaving the land he loved.

"I'm stopping at the cemetery before I leave." Zach's deep voice made Cade hesitate.

"See you there." He knew his response was barely civil, knew too that Zach would understand his foul mood wasn't aimed at him or his brothers. He slid behind the wheel and twisted the ignition key.

The four trucks left the Triple C ranch yard single file, heading for Indian Springs, the nearest town.

A half hour later, Cade stood with his three younger brothers, hat in hand, head bowed, at their mother's graveside in the Indian Springs cemetery.

Cade was the last to say goodbye, bending to lay a bouquet of daisies, Melanie Coulter's favorite flower, next to her headstone.

"Bye, Mom," he murmured, fighting back the wave of guilt, regret and sadness that always accompanied thoughts of his mother. He trailed his fingertips over the cool marble headstone and turned away, settling his Stetson on his head as he joined his brothers. His gaze flicked over the other three, struck as always by the family resemblance. They'd inherited their mother's green eyes, although her sons all had different shades from jade to bright emerald. Their six-foot-plus height, broad shoulders and black hair, however, had clearly been passed on to them by their father.

"I guess this is it," Cade said. He ignored the lump in his throat and pulled Zach into a hard hug. "You take care. Don't get yourself killed taking some damn fool risk."

Zach shook his head, lips curving in a faint smile. "You know me, Cade. I can't resist a challenge."

"Yeah, well just make sure some challenge doesn't end your life."

"I'm not the one joining the Marines," Zach reminded him. "Or riding rodeo bulls like Brodie." He slung one arm over his youngest brother's shoulders. "Eli and I are the only two planning on having normal jobs—I'm off to college and he's interning with a silversmith in Santa Fe." He pointed a finger at Cade. "You and Brodie are far more likely to get yourselves killed than we are."

"Maybe," Cade drawled, a rare grin breaking over his face. "But you've got Mom's thrillseeker gene, which means you could get yourself killed any day, anywhere."

Zach shrugged. He couldn't deny he loved to take risks.

Cade glanced at his wristwatch. "I've got to go or I'll miss my appointment with the recruiter in Billings. You guys know my cell phone number. I'll let you know when I'm out of boot camp. We'll keep in touch."

He met each of his brothers' solemn gazes, waiting until each nodded their agreement, acknowledging they were making a promise.

"We'll keep in touch," Zach repeated.

Eli and Brodie echoed the words.

Barely five minutes later, Cade drove south, away from Indian Springs, his brothers and the Triple C ranch he loved, away from the father whose grief-stricken descent into alcoholism after their mother's death had made his life a living hell for the past ten years.

He knew he'd never be back.

Chapter One

Early March
Indian Springs, Montana

Mariah Jones shoved open the barn door and braced herself for the frigid bite of a March Montana day. The wind swept down from the buttes, carrying the chilly scent of snow, and she tucked her chin deeper into the shelter of her coat collar. Despite the pale sunshine and the protection of her fleece-lined coat, gloves and wool hat, she couldn't escape the sting of cold.

She walked to the corral and upended a bucket of oats into the metal feeder just inside the pole fence. A longlegged sorrel quarterhorse left the shelter of the cattle shed across the pen and ambled toward her.

"Hey, Sarge," Mariah crooned. The big gelding eyed her, his liquid brown eyes inquisitive, and she tugged off one glove to stroke her bare palm over his soft muzzle. He nickered, pushing against her hand and snorting softly before he lowered his head to the pile of grain.

Mariah rubbed Sarge's neck beneath the rough tangle of his dark mane, drawing comfort from the gelding's easy acceptance and the feel of his solid, warm body beneath her palm. She still had a long list of chores to finish before she could rest, but the familiar crunch of oats between the horse's strong teeth and the inevitable signs of winter moving toward spring soothed the worry that nagged at her, stilling her for the moment. There was reassurance in the ordinary moments of ranch life—especially now, when the rhythm of life on the Triple C had changed irrevocably only a few months earlier.

She petted Sarge's neck in absentminded movements, distracted as her gaze moved over the buildings that made up the Triple C headquarters. Across the wide gravel yard, the two-story structure of the main house was silent. There was no trail of smoke drifting skyward from the chimney, no movement behind the drawn curtains. The house looked shuttered and lifeless.

Grief caught her unaware, slicing into her heart with all the power of a razor-sharp knife. Her lips trembled and her vision blurred before she firmed her chin, willing the tears not to fall. Three months had passed since Joseph Coulter, owner of the Triple C, had died of lung cancer. They'd buried him in the small family plot in Indian Springs Cemetery, next to his wife and among the graves of generations of Coulters that had cared for the ranch before him.

"I miss him, Sarge," she murmured, turning her face away from the deep porch, now so empty without Joseph's gray-haired, lanky figure. The taciturn sixty-eight-year-old widower had become a father figure to Mariah and his passing had left a deep ache in her heart.

Everything seems quieter, she thought as her gaze slipped over the cluster of outbuildings, corrals and the big barn. She had the strange sense that the Coulter Cattle Company was holding its breath, marking time while waiting for the next generation of Coulter males to arrive and set it in motion once again.

The rumble of an engine broke the quiet. Mariah looked up just as a mud-spattered pickup rattled over the planks of the bridge across the creek. Moments later, the driver pulled up next to the corral and got out to join her at the fence.

"Any news?" she asked hopefully, searching the older ranch hand's somber features.

Pete Smith shook his head, his weathered face doleful beneath the battered cowboy hat he wore. "Ned says the detective agency hasn't found them yet."

"Do they have any leads?"

"No."

Mariah nearly groaned aloud. Ned Anderson, the local attorney representing the Coulter estate, had been unable to locate the heirs. A month ago, he'd hired a Denver detective agency to take over the search but Joseph's four sons were proving surprisingly difficult to find.

"I realize it's been more than a dozen years since Joseph had any contact with them but still, how is it possible for four men to disappear so thoroughly?" she said, frustration coloring her tone.

"I don't know, Mariah." Pete lifted the worn hat and rubbed gnarled fingers over his close-cropped white hair. Worry furrowed his brow. "I heard gossip over the years that said them boys made a pact. The older ones waited until the youngest was done with high school and they all left the next day. They swore they'd never come back to the Triple C but nobody ever said where they went when they left."

"I hope they're found soon." Mariah's salary and tips as a waitress at the diner in Indian Springs barely covered food and necessities. The feed store was running a tab for hay and grain but she had no idea how long they would continue to do so. And after months of medical expenses, Joseph's bank account had been nearly empty when he died.

"Me too, Mariah, me too." Pete awkwardly patted her shoulder, then clapped his hat on his head and jerked a thumb at the truck. "I'll carry the groceries in before I get back to work on the tractor."

The wind picked up and Mariah shivered as the two carried bags to the bunkhouse kitchen. The Triple C had been a haven for all three of them—Pete, fellow ranch hand J.T. and herself—when they each had desperately needed shelter. They'd vowed to remain and care for it until Joseph's sons returned to take over. She knew all of them privately hoped to stay on. But the ranch belonged to the Coulter heirs—she could only pray they were found soon.

Mid-March
Mexico

The sixteenth day of March was unseasonably hot, even for the arid acres of the Rancho del Oro, located deep in the Mexican state of Chihuahua.

Cade Coulter tossed a roll of barbed wire into the back of the dusty ranch truck and walked to the cab. He reached through the open window and grabbed a thermal jug from the passenger seat. With one easy gesture, he unscrewed the lid and tilted his head back to drink. The cold water washed the dust from his throat and he didn't stop swallowing until the jug was nearly empty.

It's too damned hot, he thought as he wiped his forearm across his brow. The aviator sunglasses he wore blocked some of the sun's rays but not all. He tugged his Stetson lower to further shade his eyes from the sun's glare and leaned against the truck's dented fender. A memory of brisk, chilly air in Montana's early spring intruded but with the ease of long practice, he ignored it, focusing on the present.

A hundred degrees in March. It's going to be hotter than the hinges of hell by midsummer. He studied the pasture inside the fence break he'd just repaired, assessing the barely visible green in the arid landscape. Under the best of circumstances, the desert-dry land offered scant feed for cattle but the winter had been even drier than usual and the land was showing the effects.

Maybe it was time to head north for the spring and summer—Utah, Idaho, maybe Wyoming, or even Canada. In the three years since he'd left the Marines, he'd worked on a series of ranches, spending summers in northern states and heading south to Mexico for the winter. There was always work for a man who knew his way around cows and horses, especially if he didn't care whether he spent weeks on the range, far away from towns and the company of other humans.

A plume of dust moved toward him down the dirt track that followed the floor of the cactus-dotted valley and disappeared over a rise several miles away. This was the first time in the two weeks he'd been sleeping at the line camp and riding fence that he'd seen signs of life beyond the occasional steer, jackrabbit or coyote.

The del Oro bordered an area with active bands of rebels—unexpected visitors were always suspect. Cade leaned into the pickup through the open window, set the gallon water jug on the seat and took a loaded rifle from the rack mounted over the back window.

Friend or foe, it paid to be ready for anything. Especially when a man spent his days this far from civilization. Fortunately, he wouldn't need to use the gun, as the truck drew nearer and he recognized a young employee from ranch headquarters.

"Hey, Cade," Kenny called as he braked to a stop, dust swirling around the dirty pickup truck with the ranch logo on the door. "I've been looking for you since yesterday."

"Yeah? Why?"

"You got a letter from an attorney in the States. Boss thought it might be important so he sent me out with it."

Cade cradled the rifle as he took the envelope, glanced at the return address and felt his blood run cold. The last bitter, angry words his father had said to him rang in Cade's mind as clearly as if Joseph Coulter had uttered them yesterday instead of thirteen years ago. *If you leave, don't come back—not until you get a letter from my lawyer telling you I'm dead.*

The words brought an instant memory of his departure from the ranch, the rearview mirror reflecting three pickup trucks following him, each driven by one of his younger brothers.

Did they know Joseph Coulter was dead?

No, Cade thought with instant certainty. He hadn't heard from any of them in several months and they would have contacted him immediately if they had learned of the news.

"Ain't you gonna read it?"

Cade realized the young cowhand had stepped out of the truck and was eyeing him expectantly.

He ripped open the envelope and unfolded the single sheet of paper, swiftly read the short paragraph, then refolded and tucked the brief message back into the envelope.

"Well? Was it important?"

"Yeah." Cade tucked the letter into his shirt pocket. "I need to pick up my horse and gear at the line camp. Tell the boss I'll be in late tonight to collect my wages before I head north."

"Damn, that letter was bad news, wasn't it?" Kenny seemed genuinely sympathetic.

Cade didn't do touchy-feely emotional stuff but something about the kid's worried face made him relent.

"My father passed away."

"I'm sorry, man. That's hard."

Cade shrugged. "It happens."

"So you have to go back home to take care of stuff for your mom?"

"My mother died when I was a kid." Cade reached into the truck and slid the rifle into the window rack.

"Damn. I'm sorry."

"Again, not your problem." Cade took pity on the kid, who looked as gloomy as if he were personally responsible for Cade's parents having died. "I appreciate you coming all the way out here to tell me."

"Sure."

Cade drove off; a brief glance in the rearview mirror told him the kid was still staring after him before he topped a rise and dropped down the other side, heading for the line camp.

With his customary efficiency, Cade packed, collected his last check and drove north toward the border. The shock of learning his father had died was numbing. But once he was on the road with little to distract him but the empty highway stretching ahead of him, the shock quickly gave way to a riptide of emotions. Anger warred with an unexpected searing regret. He hadn't seen his father for thirteen years. He shouldn't care that the man was dead. But a leaden weight pressed on his chest and, despite a gut-deep rejection of the emotion, Cade remembered feeling that same heaviness after his mother died. He had an uneasy suspicion the pressure was caused by grief.

Cade tried to reach his brothers but none of the three answered their cell phones. He left brief messages for each asking them to return his call as soon as they could. He didn't tell them their father had passed away—he figured he'd wait until he had more information. The attorney's letter hadn't listed details, only that Joseph Coulter had died and the law office needed to speak with Cade, in person, as soon as possible. Since it wasn't likely Joseph Coulter had left any of his assets to either Cade or his brothers, Cade suspected he might be able to resolve any questions from the attorney without Zach, Brodie or Eli having to make the trip home.

He doubted he'd be in Indian Springs more than a few days. He planned to visit the attorney to take care of whatever small bit of business the man needed from him, stop by his mother's grave, say hello to a couple old friends before leaving town. He'd worked on a ranch near Cody, Wyoming, the year before and the owner had told him when he left that he had a job any time he wanted. Wyoming would be a good place to spend the summer.

He didn't respond to the attorney's letter with a phone call or note. Instead, he packed his truck, loaded his horse, Jiggs, into the trailer and headed north. It took almost a week of driving from dawn to dusk before he crossed the Montana state line. The farther north he drove, the chillier the weather grew. Full spring had yet to arrive in northeastern Montana and snow lay deep in coulees, whitened the ruts between plowed black rows in wheat fields, and filled the roadside ditches.

Five days after leaving Del Oro, in midafternoon, he turned off the highway and onto the gravel road that led to the ranch headquarters, driving beneath the familiar welded arch. The graceful curves of ironwork spelled out "Coulter Cattle Company," the heavy metal frame standing tall and sturdy although the once-bright paint was worn away. The road stretched between fenced pastures where an occasional Hereford steer or a horse with its shaggy winter coat peered at him over the top strand of barbed wire fences.

The road curved around the base of a butte and climbed a rise. From the top, Cade saw the buildings that he'd once called home, clustered at the foot of a flat-topped hill on the far side of the valley.

He wasn't sure what he was supposed to feel after thirteen years but he hadn't expected to feel numb.

Maybe he'd been gone too long. Maybe the roots that once held him here were well and truly dead.

Or maybe I've been driving too long with too little sleep, he thought.

The truck and horse trailer rattled over the old bridge spanning the creek, then climbed the slope to the buildings. Cade pulled up the truck next to the corral and barn and stepped out. Rolling his shoulders to ease the tension of days spent driving, he turned in a slow circle, scanning the buildings.

The house needed a coat of paint and held an air of abandonment, its curtains drawn behind blank windows. The barn with its low cattle shed attached at one end, the granaries and machine shop were all weather-beaten. What little paint remained on the structures was peeling from the gray boards. All the buildings looked down-at-the-heels rough but Cade's assessing gaze found no sagging rooflines. The structures appeared to be square and solid on their foundations.

Jiggs stamped and shifted, rocking the trailer on its axles and demanding attention.

Cade walked to the back of the trailer, unlocked and swung the gate wide. Jiggs looked over his shoulder and gave an impatient huff.

"Hey, boy." Cade grinned, entering the trailer and moving past the big stud to untie him. "Little anxious to get out of here?" The horse shifted his weight and nudged Cade's shoulder with his nose. "I don't blame you. It's been a long trip."

He caught the lead rope at the halter, just under the black's muzzle. "Back up, big guy."

Jiggs obeyed, his hooves clattering on the wooden trailer deck. The minute all four feet were on solid ground, he shook himself and danced in a half circle at the end of the lead rope, lifting his head to look around. His ears pricked forward and he whinnied.

Cade looked over his shoulder to see what had caught Jiggs's interest, turning fully when he saw a young woman standing just outside the open barn door, a bucket of grain in one hand. Silvery blond hair brushed the shoulders of a dark green barn coat and her brown eyes were wide, the surprise on her oval face clearly indicating she hadn't expected to see him. She wore faded jeans beneath the bulky coat and old boots covered her feet, her walk smooth and graceful as she moved toward him.

His eyes narrowed as he tried to place her and failed. If she was a neighbor, he didn't remember her.

And I would have remembered, he thought. Even covered by the coat and plain jeans, he could tell her body was slim and curved. Her fair skin glowed with health in the weak afternoon sunlight, her mouth lush below a small, straight nose. And her thick-lashed brown eyes were alive with intelligence, curiosity and a feminine interest mixed with wariness.

Everything male in him noticed—and liked what he saw.

"Hello," she said, her voice slightly husky. Her gaze was fastened on his face and the small frown that veed the arch of her brows cleared as she drew nearer. "You're one of Joseph's sons, aren't you."

It wasn't a question. The conviction in her voice was strong, mixed with the relief reflected on her face.

"I'm Cade Coulter. Who are you?"

Her eyes widened when he gave his name but she didn't reply with her own. She seemed wholly absorbed in studying him and the open fascination in her deep brown eyes started slow heat simmering through his veins, his muscles tightening as her gaze swept slowly over his face and moved lower.

Mariah stared at the man in front of her. He was tall, easily a few inches over six feet, his shoulders broad beneath a sheepskin-lined tan coat. He wore a gray Stetson over coal-black hair and beneath the brim's shadow, black lashes framed his deep green eyes. He wasn't conventionally handsome but there was something essentially male, powerful and vaguely dangerous about him. His face was angular with a firm jaw, strong cheekbones, straight nose and a hard mouth.

He swept a slow, assessing look from the crown of her head to her boots and back up again. She caught her breath, awareness prickling her skin at the male heat that blazed for a brief moment in his darkened eyes before they were once again unreadable.

She realized that he'd asked her a question but she hadn't answered, too busy drinking in his dark good looks while shivers of excitement raced over her skin. Self-conscious heat warmed her cheeks and she struggled to conceal her reaction to him.

"I'm Mariah Jones," she told him. "I work here."

He stared at her for a moment, those green eyes unblinking. Then he looked away, sweeping the area with a quick glance. "Where's the rest of the crew?"

"There are only three of us—Pete Smith, J. T. Butler and me."

"Three of you?" His voice was harsh, incredulous. "For how long?"

"I've been here four years," she replied. "And J.T.

about two. I'm not sure how long Pete worked for Joseph. He was here when I arrived."

Cade let his gaze sweep over the run-down buildings once again. "No wonder this place looks like hell."

"There aren't enough hours in the day to keep up with everything," she said evenly, trying to tamp down the spurt of anger caused by his comment.

He glanced at her, lifting a brow as if surprised at the thread of defensiveness in her voice. "I didn't say there were. But this is a big ranch. Three people aren't enough manpower to do more than barely keep this place running." He flicked another glance over the buildings. "Where are the other two?"

"Pete went to town for mail and groceries. J.T. isn't due home from school for another couple of hours."

"School? How old is he?"

"Seventeen."

He swore under his breath and glared at her. "How old is Smith?"

"Sixty-five."

"A kid, a guy on Social Security and a girl. What the hell was the old man thinking?"

"If you're referring to your father, I suspect he was doing the best he could with what he had," she said, an unmistakable snap in her tone.

He gave her another dark, unreadable look. "Yeah, I expect he was." He took off his hat and ran his fingers through thick black hair, raking it from his forehead in a frustrated gesture.

Mariah had seen Joseph make that same gesture a hundred times, and the likeness between father and son was suddenly sharpened.

Cade turned away and led the big horse to the corral.

Yanking the lock bar free, he swung open the gate and walked the horse in, unsnapping the lead rope to set the animal loose. The stallion immediately trotted to the water trough and hay rack on the far side of the enclosure.

"I'm heading into town to talk to the attorney," Cade told her as he unhitched the horse trailer from the dusty truck. "I should be back in a couple of hours." He yanked open the pickup door and paused. "I've been on the road for days and I'm tired of restaurant food. Does anyone cook around here?"

"We take turns. Supper's on the table in the bunk-house at six. Tonight it's chili."

"I'll be here." The engine turned over and the pickup rolled forward, swinging in a U-turn.

Moments later, Mariah stood alone next to the empty horse trailer, watching a plume of dust rise behind the truck's wheels as it sped down the gravel lane toward the highway.

So that's Joseph's oldest son. Mariah wasn't sure exactly what she'd expected but the hard-eyed, dangerous-looking man bore only a passing resemblance to the laughing ten-year-old boy in the family portrait hanging on Joseph's wall.

And when his green eyes had briefly flickered with heat after that first slow, assessing stare, she'd burned. The brush of his gaze was as physically arousing as if he'd reached out and slowly trailed his fingers over her bare skin, from her chin to her toes and back again.

She hadn't expected to be attracted to Cade Coulter.

It was a complication she didn't want. And it was sure to cause trouble, she thought with conviction. She'd simply have to set aside her attraction, she told herself, and focus on her promise to Joseph that she would do everything she could to encourage his sons to remain on the Triple C. She was determined to fulfill her vow and see Joseph's last wish come true.

With renewed determination, she turned on her heel and walked toward the bunkhouse. She needed to start the chili simmering. She had only a few short hours until dinner—and Cade's return.

Chapter Two

A half hour after driving away from the Triple C, a beaming receptionist ushered Cade into Ned Anderson's office. The attorney rose and leaned over the gleaming surface of his desk to shake Cade's hand.

"I don't mind saying I'm damn glad to see you, Cade." The attorney waved him to a seat in one of the leather armchairs facing the desk and dropped back into his own chair. "I was beginning to wonder whether we'd be able to locate you and your brothers."

"How long have you been looking?" Cade asked, curious.

"Ever since Joseph passed away." Anderson peered at Cade over the tops of reading glasses, his eyes shrewd. "I assumed he had current addresses for all of you but discovered too late that he didn't. Do you have any up-to-date contact information for your brothers?"

"Yes." Cade took his cell phone from his coat pocket. "I can give you their cell phone numbers and last known addresses."

The attorney jotted notes on a pad as Cade read off Zach, Eli and Brodie's information. "Excellent," he said with satisfaction when Cade finished. "I'll pass this on to the investigator immediately. Hopefully he'll be able to talk to them all within a day or two."

"I wouldn't count on it."

"Why not?"

"Because I left messages on all their cell phones as soon as I got your letter. That was five days ago and none of them have checked in."

Anderson frowned. "Why not?"

Cade shrugged. "Hard to say. It's not unusual to wait awhile for an answer."

"How long is 'awhile'?"

"Depends on where everyone is." Cade noted the attorney's lack of comprehension. "None of us spends a lot of time in one place," he explained. "Brodie's a champion bull rider and follows the rodeo circuit—usually rents an apartment in a different place each year after the season ends. Eli's a silversmith—sometimes he rents a studio but often apprentices with another artist. When he's studying, he might spend a year or more living near the master teacher's studio. And Zach…" Cade paused, a half-smile curving his lips. "Actually, Zach's the one we use to keep in touch. He works for a company in San Francisco and bought a condo there years ago. He travels a lot for his job, though, and since I haven't heard from him, I'm guessing he's not in San Francisco right now."

"So you have no idea how long it may take to reach them?"

Cade shook his head. "No."

The attorney sighed and scrubbed his hands over his face. His chair squeaked as he leaned back. "That complicates matters."

"Why?" Cade asked bluntly.

"Because the Triple C is barely holding on by its fingertips and only you four Coulters can save it."

Cade's gaze narrowed as he straightened in his chair. "I don't understand."

The attorney sat forward, took a thick file from a stack on the corner of his desk and flipped it open. He sifted through documents before sliding a sheaf of papers across the desk. "This is a copy of your father's last will and testament. You'll want to read it carefully, but briefly I can tell you that, with one exception, Joseph left everything he owned to you and your three brothers."

Stunned, Cade stared at Anderson for a moment before picking up the document.

"You'll notice on page three," Anderson continued, "that Joseph left the Triple C to all of you in one-fourth shares. He also left each of you control of individual aspects of the ranch. In your case, he left you all the cattle and any other livestock. You have the power to sell any of them you want. But you can't sell the land. None of you can sell any of the Triple C acres without express consent, in writing, of the other three."

If Cade didn't have the will in front of him, he wouldn't have believed Anderson. But the document was clear. He scanned the typed pages quickly, stopping abruptly when he reached page five.

"He left my grandparents' cabin and three acres to

Mariah Jones?" The quick flash of anger echoed in his words.

"Yes." Anderson didn't flinch from Cade's hard stare. "Joseph died of cancer. Mariah Jones took care of him, and it was my observation that he viewed her as a daughter."

"I'll bet he did." Cade's growled response held sarcasm. He didn't believe any man, even one Joseph's age, could look at the blonde and not see a beautiful, sexy woman. He tossed the will onto the desk in front of him. "That cabin sits within yards of the barn and is part of Triple C headquarters, plus it's landlocked and surrounded by Coulter land. Is there a way to break the will and keep it part of the ranch?"

"No," Anderson replied. "A clause provides any heir challenging any part of the will shall have their portion of the estate gifted to the State of Montana's park system."

Cade frowned, silently considering the problem before deciding to shelve it for the moment. Not that he believed there wasn't a way to keep the cabin in Coulter hands, nor that Mariah Jones hadn't somehow manipulated Joseph to convince him to leave her the valuable property. The cabin was important not only because of its location—his grandfather had built it with his own hands. It was part of Coulter history and he'd find a way to reclaim it. "You said the ranch is hanging on by its fingertips. What do you mean?" he asked, returning to the larger issue of the Triple C.

"There are no cash assets. Joseph was increasingly ill for several years and medical bills ate up what cash he had. The ranch itself has been maintained but not at optimum level."

Cade nodded. "I went to the Triple C before coming here. I've seen the buildings though I haven't closely assessed them."

"Then you have some idea of what you're up against," Ned replied. He slid another document across the desktop to Cade. "This is information about the inheritance taxes. As you can see, they're substantial and are the most pressing problem you and your brothers will have. Unless any of you are independently wealthy and have the means to pay them?" he added, a hopeful note in his voice.

The total tax dollars owed was staggering.

"No," Cade replied. "We're all solvent but I doubt any of us has that kind of money."

"Then you'll have to work together to find a way to make the ranch earn enough to pay the taxes." Ned eyed Cade.

"It'll take a damned miracle," Cade told him.

"Perhaps." The attorney replied.

"Is there anything else I need to know right now?" Cade asked.

"I think you have the basics."

"Then I'll head back to the ranch." Cade stood and held out his hand, shaking the attorney's as he stood. "I'll be in touch."

"Good. And Cade…"

Cade paused at the doorway to look back at Anderson.

"Welcome home."

Cade nodded and left the office.

Barely two hours after he'd left Mariah in the ranch yard, Cade drove out of Indian Springs and headed back to the Triple C. His discussion with the attorney about the details of his father's estate had raised more questions than answers.

Given the long estrangement between Cade, his brothers and their father, Cade hadn't expected any of them to receive much, if anything, from his estate. To his surprise, Joseph Coulter had left nearly everything he owned to his four sons in approximately equal shares.

But the Triple C had barely been making ends meet before Joseph's death, Cade thought grimly, and there was a good chance his sons would lose the vast acres to taxes and debt.

And just to add to the complicated mess his father had left for his sons to sort out, Joseph had given his grandparents' cabin to Mariah Jones. The house and its acre of surrounding land edged the creek bank and sat within view of the main ranch house, just beyond the barn and outbuildings. The blonde also had a legal right to use the lane to the highway.

Unless he could find a way to break that part of his father's will, Cade was stuck with having Mariah living on the ranch permanently.

It was almost six o'clock and full dark when he reached the Triple C. His headlights arced over the corral and barn before he parked in front of the bunkhouse where warm lamplight poured through the windows. At the main house across the ranch yard, only the solitary porch light glowed, throwing the ends of the deep porch into shadow.

Cade climbed the shallow steps to the bunkhouse and entered without knocking.

The three people seated at the table in the kitchen area all looked up. Two men, one older and one kid, sat with Mariah, whose hair gleamed silver in the light. Her brown eyes widened before her expression shuttered.

"Evening," Cade said, hanging his hat on a hook next to the door and shrugging out of his coat.

"Hello." Mariah pushed back her chair and walked to the stove. She picked up potholders, pausing to look over her shoulder. "J.T., Pete, this is Cade Coulter."

The two stood as Cade joined them.

"Evenin', boss." The elderly cowboy was lean and rangy, shoulders slightly stooped. A white shock of hair covered his head and bright blue eyes were shrewd under heavy eyebrows. His lined face with its craggy nose and strong chin held character and gave testimony to a lifetime of working outside in Montana weather.

"Evening, boss." The kid's greeting copied the older man's right down to the inflection and polite neutrality. He was equally tall and rangy except his shoulders were square, straight with youth. His dark blond hair was a shade too long and brushed his collar in back, his navy blue eyes cool and unreadable as they met Cade's. He wore faded jeans, cowboy boots and a ripped but clean plaid flannel shirt that hung unbuttoned over a black T-shirt. The tee had a faded rock band logo with the words "hell-raiser" centered on his chest.

The three men shook hands, murmured polite hellos, before they all sat down. Cade caught a glimpse of a tattoo just beneath the edge of the shirt's worn neckline as J.T. sat.

The kid's got attitude, Cade thought. *I wonder if he's any good at working on a ranch.*

"Corn bread is on the plate, under the cover." Mariah set a steaming bowl of chili in front of Cade, nodding at the red gingham covered dish in the center of the table.

"Thanks." Cade breathed in a faint floral scent as she leaned closer to lower the bowl before she moved away. He felt his muscles tighten and he had to restrain the urge to watch the sway of her hips encased in faded jeans. She wore a sweater with a high neck, her hair a spill of silvery blond against the bright red wool. She was covered from head to toe in boots, jeans and wool sweater yet she drew his attention like a magnet.

"Careful, the bowl's hot," she commented before she returned to her seat across the table.

They ate in silence, emptying their bowls and the plate of corn bread. Pete carried his china and utensils to the sink and returned with a thermal carafe of coffee, gnarled fingers holding the handles of four mugs. He poured and passed around filled mugs without saying a word.

"Thanks." Cade sipped his coffee and leaned back in the wooden chair. "Suppose you all bring me up-to-date on what's been happening here." He glanced around the table. "Who's in charge of the cattle?"

"I guess that would be me," Pete said in his gravelly voice. "Though we all pitch in with fixing fences or moving a herd when necessary."

"How many cow-calf pairs was Dad running? How many steers? And how many did you lose over the winter?"

Pete quoted numbers that surprised Cade. "That's more cattle than I'd expected, especially with just three full-time hands."

"Two full-time hands," Pete corrected him. "Mariah only works here part-time."

Cade's eyes narrowed over the slender female. She met his gaze without comment. He couldn't help wondering why Joseph had left a valuable house to a part-time employee. Cynicism told him there had to be a reason and more than likely, the answer wouldn't make him happy or reflect favorably on the pretty blonde. He shifted in his seat, annoyed that he was attracted to the woman who may have conned and used his father.

"And Mariah is most likely the reason we've got such a low loss rate," Pete said with pride. "She keeps track of the baby calves and makes sure they survive the first few weeks. She usually ropes J.T. into helping her so I guess he deserves some of the credit, too."

"My thanks to you both." Cade's words only brought a nod of acceptance from Mariah but the teenager shifted in his seat, faint streaks of red marking his cheekbones, clearly uncomfortable with both Pete's praise and Cade's thanks.

"What about other livestock?" Cade queried.

"There's not much," Pete told him. "A few saddle horses, a mule or two, and some chickens Joseph kept for the eggs."

Cade considered the news. "So what you're telling me is that the ranch is running cattle, but not much else?"

Pete exchanged glances with Mariah and J.T., then nodded.

"What about field crops? I noticed alfalfa bales stacked and tarped in the flat next to the creek this afternoon. Was Dad planting oats or rye in the fields bordering the highway?"

"Joseph stopped planting anything but alfalfa several years ago," Pete told him. "Said he just couldn't keep up with the work and he'd rather raise cattle."

Cade wondered how long the old man had been sick but didn't ask. "And the Kigers? Are they still on Tunk Mountain?"

Pete, J.T. and Mariah all wore identical expressions of blank confusion.

"The Kigers?" J.T. repeated, stressing the last word rhyming with *tiger* as if the word were part of a foreign language. "What are Kigers?"

"Mustangs," Cade said. "My mother bred and raised them."

Pete shrugged. "I never heard Joseph mention them. Ain't never been to Tunk Mountain, either. We kept the cattle closer to home." He frowned. "Don't remember chasing cattle on Tunk Mountain for roundup, either, come to think of it." His shrewd blue eyes fixed on Cade. "If Joseph had a herd of horses on the mountain, he kept it a secret."

Cade shrugged. "Maybe he sold them years ago."

"If you don't mind me asking, boss," Pete began, "we were wondering what plans you have for the Triple C?"

"I'll try to hold it together and pay the bills until my brothers are located and can get here," he said brusquely, his tone grim. He hadn't missed the tension that instantly gripped all three when Pete asked his question. He wasn't going to lie or sugarcoat the truth. They'd stayed on the ranch without wages when they could have sought work elsewhere and they deserved nothing less than his honesty. "From what the attorney told me about the ranch's financial situation, that won't be easy."

"And what happens when your brothers arrive?" Mariah asked.

"I guess we'll decide if we're going to sell out or try

to hold the Triple C permanently." He glanced at his wristwatch. "It's been a long day. I think I'll check on Jiggs and head up to the house."

"If Jiggs is the black, I fed and watered him, then put him in a stall in the barn," J.T. told him. "He's not a quarterhorse, is he?"

"He's Andalusian," Cade explained. "I brought him home with me from Spain." The look on the kid's face told Cade that he was burning to ask questions, probably lots of questions, but Cade wasn't in the mood to give him answers. He shoved back his chair and stood, carrying his bowl and utensils to the sink before recrossing the room to collect his hat and coat.

"The attorney told me the estate hasn't paid salaries since the old man died," Cade said as he shrugged into his coat. "I'll have to look at the books before paying you whatever salary you're owed but if anyone needs an advance for the next few days, I have cash."

Relief lit the two men's expressions.

"I'm almost out of pipe tobacco. I could use fifty," Pete told him.

"Me, too," J.T. added.

"I can wait until you've had time to review the payroll accounts," Mariah said. "They're on Joseph's desk in his office."

Cade nodded and took out his wallet, counting out bills before handing them to Pete and J.T.

"Who's been doing the bookkeeping?" he asked, sweeping a glance over the three.

"Mariah," Pete answered, gesturing at her. "She's better at math than I am."

"Better than me, too," J.T. put in.

Mariah tucked her hair behind her ear and didn't

comment. Cade's face had tightened at the other men's comments and she didn't have to be a mind reader to guess that her new boss wasn't happy she'd been the one keeping track of the ranch's financial records.

"Come up to the house tomorrow morning," Cade told her. "You can explain the system to me."

"I'm at the café until eleven but I should be home by noon."

He frowned. "You're eating breakfast in town?"

"No, I have the early shift tomorrow."

"You're working in town and here—holding down two jobs?" His stare was piercing.

She nodded but didn't elaborate further. She wasn't going to explain that without her waitress job, the three of them—her, Pete and J.T.—would have gone hungry over the last few months.

Fortunately, Cade didn't ask any more questions.

"All right, stop in when you get back," he said tersely.

She swallowed a sigh of relief. "Sounds good. If there's nothing else you need me for tonight, I'll head for home. I have to be up at four o'clock."

"No," he said brusquely. "There's nothing else."

She said good-night and slipped into her coat, tugging on gloves as she stepped outside and halted on the porch to pull on a knit hat. To her surprise, Cade joined her, pulling the door closed behind him, shutting Pete and J.T. inside.

Mariah glanced up at him, his face shadowy beneath the brim of his hat. "I turned up the heat in the ranch house earlier. We've kept the furnace set on low so the pipes wouldn't freeze but it wasn't enough to keep the rooms warm enough to be comfortable. And I put clean sheets on the bed in the front corner room upstairs," she added.

Cade glanced at her sharply. "Thanks," he said.

Her brown eyes searched his. "You're upset that Joseph left me the house by the creek," she said with calm certainty.

Anger flared over the hard lines of his face but quickly disappeared.

"I'm more interested in *why* he left it to you. It's surrounded by Coulter acres and essentially landlocked."

"Yes." She nodded. "I have to drive past your house to get to the highway. Joseph said he was going to give it to me so I'd always have a home." Because Joseph had known how badly she needed a place to belong, she thought. She'd drifted without an anchor in the years after her father died, the home of her childhood sold to pay medical bills long before his death.

"And what did you do for him that earned you a house?" His voice was toneless yet Mariah felt his cynicism.

She stiffened. "I rode fence, cared for newborn calves, cooked meals and valued his friendship. Joseph Coulter was a second father to me. He treated me with kindness, respect and consideration." Her voice was cool but a thread of anger ran beneath her words.

"Good to know he was a kind father to somebody."

The implication that Joseph hadn't been one to his own sons was obvious.

"I'm sorry if you didn't feel the same about him," she said stiffly.

"I didn't." Cade was blunt. "He was a mean drunk who took his misery out on his sons. He started drinking after my mother died and got worse with each year that passed. As soon as Eli finished high school, we all left home to get away from him. So, no, it's fair to say Joseph Coulter never treated me or my brothers with kindness or respect."

Mariah caught her breath, stunned by the harsh words. She was more shocked, however, by the lack of emotion in Cade's voice. He was as casual as if he were telling her his favorite food was a cheeseburger and fries. "That's not the Joseph Coulter I knew," she said softly. "He never drank during the years I worked here. I'm sorry."

"Why should you be sorry—it wasn't your fault." He waved a hand at the two shallow steps. "I'll walk you to the cabin."

"You don't have to," she protested. "I walk home every night on my own."

"Well, now I'm here and you don't have to walk alone." His tone brooked no argument.

"Very well." Mariah gave in and moved down the steps ahead of him. As they followed the gravel road past the barn toward the creek and the cabin tucked into the trees, she was vividly aware of the big man prowling beside her. "Where did Ned Anderson finally locate you?" she asked, curious.

"Mexico," he replied, turning his head to look at her.

"Really?" She met his gaze with surprise before her mouth curved in amusement. "I'm guessing you weren't happy about leaving the warmth of Mexico for a chilly March in Montana."

"It was already getting hot there," he said. "Too hot."

"What part of Mexico were you in?"

"Chihuahua. I was working on a ranch—riding fence, working cattle." He glanced around them, his gaze sweeping the moonlit pasture beyond the creek. "It's a relief to be farther north with weather cold enough that I'll need a jacket."

Mariah couldn't help but smile at the satisfaction behind his words. "I hope that means you'll stay here in Montana, on the ranch."

"I was born and raised here." He turned his head, his gaze sweeping the horizon. "I'd like to stay on this land—maybe see my nieces or nephews grow up here."

"Nephews or nieces?" Curious, she searched his profile, etched by moonlight against the darker shadows of night. "Not your own son or daughter?"

"I'll never have kids."

His flat statement surprised her. "You sound very sure," she replied, curious.

"I am."

She stared at him. "You don't like children?"

He shrugged. "I like kids. But given who my father was, I'm not taking any chances I might turn out like him." He caught her arm when she stumbled. "Careful."

His big hand cupped her elbow but he released her as soon as she steadied. She wished he hadn't—the contact was electric and exhilarating, distracting her from his comment about Joseph. They reached the cabin and she climbed the steps, pausing at the door to turn and face him.

"Thanks for walking me home."

He touched the brim of his hat. "My pleasure."

Mariah felt the faintly gravelly tones of his drawl

shiver over her skin and for a moment, she thought, hoped, he would say more. But then he turned and strode down the steps.

"Good night," she called. He didn't turn, merely lifted a hand in response and kept walking. His tall, broad-shouldered figure was a dark silhouette against the paler gravel until the road curved to the left and Cade disappeared in the deeper shadow cast by the barn.

Mariah sighed unconsciously and entered the house. She'd spent only an hour or so in his company yet Cade Coulter made her foolish body respond with shivers and undeniable excitement.

Of all the men in the world, she thought, why him? He had every reason to resent her after Joseph had made her an heir. But Joseph had dreamed of having his sons back on the Triple C and she was committed to helping that dream come true, despite Cade's suspicions as to her motives. Cade hadn't actually accused her of scamming his father but his skepticism about her response as to why Joseph had left her the house had been clear.

Cade couldn't be more wrong about her, she thought. She would never have tried to manipulate or harm Joseph—she owed him too much to ever betray him.

A few years earlier, she'd taken a break from college classes and set out on a driving tour through Montana. She didn't know exactly where she caught the flu virus, but she'd become violently ill on the road and while trying to reach Indian Springs, had passed out, losing control of her car. The vehicle had ended up in the ditch just past the Triple C ranch turnoff and Joseph had taken her in. He'd called a doctor, then he and Pete had tended her until she recovered from a raging fever and gut-wrenching flu symptoms. A year later, when her apartment building in Indian Springs burned to the ground, the solitary rancher had offered her a home in a vacant cabin on the Triple C. The more time she spent with the quiet, sad man, the more she grew to like him and when he'd been diagnosed with cancer, there was no question that she'd care for him as if he were her own father.

She'd never expected payment for being kind to him. She'd often told him it was her privilege to ease his last days on earth. She had no other family and knowing Joseph felt a paternal affection for her warmed her heart and enriched her life.

No, she told herself with conviction, if Joseph hadn't welcomed her into his life on the Triple C along with Pete and J.T., she would have been alone.

It was impossible to imagine Joseph harming his sons, yet Cade's comments about his father had rang with truth.

If she accepted Cade's damning statement, she felt disloyal to Joseph.

If she hadn't dearly loved the old man, she thought, she'd pack her bags, turn over the house keys to Joseph's oldest son, and move into town.

But she *had* loved Joseph. So she'd guard her tongue and swallow angry replies—at least until Cade had time to grow familiar with the workings of the Triple C.

She sighed and made her way to bed but sleep eluded her and she lay awake much too long, pondering and worrying about the changes that were sure to follow Cade's return to the Triple C.

Chapter Three

After leaving Mariah at her cabin, Cade kept walking, past the bunkhouse to the barn. He'd been caught off guard by the urge to bend his head and taste her mouth. He hadn't been tempted to act impulsively with a woman since he was a kid and he couldn't help fantasizing about what she'd look like out of those snug, faded jeans.

He stopped to look in on Jiggs, entering the barn through a small door to the right of the bigger, wide-plank door. Overhead lights flashed on with the flick of the switch just inside the door and Jiggs lifted his muzzle from a water pail, nickering when he saw Cade.

"Hey, boy." Cade ran a quick assessing gaze over the black's quarters. Fresh straw bedding covered the floor of the box stall. The manger was filled with hay and Jiggs looked happy and content. He made a mental note to thank J.T. "Looks like the kid treated you right."

Jiggs bobbed his head up and down before he nuzzled Cade's jacket pocket.

"Sorry," Cade told him. "No apples tonight. I forgot to buy any in town. I'll get some tomorrow."

Jiggs *whuffed* in disappointment. Cade chuckled and smoothed his palm down the black's face and muzzle.

"You're spoiled." He patted the black's strong neck and turned away. He looked back just before he snapped off the light and grinned at the horse's disappointed expression.

Cade left the barn and crossed the ranch yard. He'd put off entering the house for as long as he could. Automatically, he scraped mud from his boots before going inside. He closed the door behind him, flipped the light switch on the wall to his right and halted, pausing to sweep the big main room with an assessing glance.

It looked the same. In fact, he thought, it was as if the house were frozen in time. The worn leather sofa and matching big chair with its ottoman were scuffed and worn but still solid and familiar. Above the huge fireplace, the heavy oak plank that his father had used to create the mantel still held a collection of framed photos and two glass oil lamps. Several stacks of magazines and books were neatly spaced atop the carved oak coffee table in front of the sofa. A small table with a lamp sat next to the cherrywood sewing rocker beside the hearth.

He crossed the room to the fireplace and with one hand, set the rocker moving gently back and forth. For a long moment, he stared at the four framed photographs before he picked up the largest, an 8 x 10 studio photo of his family. His mother's green eyes glowed with the same happiness that curved her mouth in a smile. His father's arm was slung over her shoulder, tucking her protectively against his side. Cade and his three brothers were little-boy stairsteps ranged in front of their parents. Melanie Coulter's hand rested on Cade's shoulder.

Cade could feel his mother's warm, loving touch as if the Coulter family had posed for the portrait only yesterday. An old, familiar pain burned in his gut and he absentmindedly rubbed his chest, just to the left of center. When he realized what he was doing, he jerked his hand away and set the photo back on the mantel.

Maybe I'm not as immune to memories as I thought.

He rolled his shoulders, shrugging off the unwelcome introspection, and turned his back on the collection of photographs, striding across the room to enter the kitchen. Here, too, time seemed to have stood still. In the far corner, the heavy wooden chair with scarred legs was pushed neatly up to the long kitchen table. Cade remembered too well how his mother had loved the table and chairs, a gift from husband and sons for her birthday. After she died, the table had grown dusty and lost its polish, the chairs earning scars from her sons' spurs knocking into the carved legs.

He shrugged out of his coat and hung it over the back of a chair, hooking his hat on the corner. He gave the room one last cursory survey, checked to make sure the coffee canister was nearly full in the cabinet above the coffeemaker next to the sink, and left the room.

Joseph Coulter's office was just down the hall from the living room. Cade pushed open the door, flipped on the light switch and stepped inside.

The big desk faced the door. Cade walked across the room and behind it, pausing to scan the framed map of the Triple C and surrounding ranches that hung on the wall. The boundaries of the huge ranch were etched in solid black.

Cade was struck anew at his father's obvious determination to hold the land. Given the financial straits the ranch was in, he knew Joseph must have been strapped for cash.

And judging by how little paint remained on the shabby buildings, he thought grimly, the Triple C had probably been running on short rations for a long time.

He dropped into the worn leather seat of the wooden swivel desk chair. The desktop was free of dust and a black accounting ledger was centered on the blotter. Three sharpened pencils, a blue ink pen, a red ink pen and a short ruler were tucked into a heavy pottery mug sitting to one side of the blotter.

Everything was clean and very neat. Cade guessed Mariah was probably responsible for the tidy house.

He flipped the ledger open to the latest entries, neat columns in red and black ink. The red ink column was much longer than the black.

Restless and unwilling to begin what was sure to be a grim review of the Triple C's finances, Cade closed the ledger and shoved back the chair. The books could wait until morning. He left the room to collect his coat and walk to his truck. The temperature had dropped since he'd come inside and a slight breeze chilled his bare face and hands, ruffling his hair. It took only moments to collect his duffel bag from his truck cab and he jogged back to the house, entering the warm living room. He hung his coat on the pegs just inside the front door before climbing the staircase to the house's second floor.

The banister was worn smooth as silk beneath his palm. Cade had a swift mental image of his mother laughing as he and his brothers slid down into his father's waiting arms. Joseph had caught and deposited each of them with swift efficiency, then lectured them sternly about the danger of falling. But his mouth had twitched with a smile as he warned them, just before he picked them up and packed them into the living room to wrestle in front of the fire.

The world had been a different, happier place before his mother died and Joseph started drinking.

Ten years of watching his father try to drown his grief in a bottle had taught Cade two unforgettable lessons. First, he was never getting married because a man in love could be sucked into hell if he lost the woman. And second, he was never having kids. Because what was the likelihood he wouldn't repeat his father's mistakes?

There are too many ghosts in this house, he thought grimly as he started down the upstairs hall.

Five closed doors lined the hallway and Cade automatically strode to the far end before turning the knob and entering the room.

He halted abruptly, his gaze slowly sweeping the room. Like the rest of the house, his childhood bedroom seemed caught in a time warp, preserved just as it was the last time he'd walked out, closed the door and left the Triple C all those years ago. Too tired to deal with the wash of emotions, he slammed the door on the sadness, regret and memories to focus on the old-fashioned brass bed, made up with fresh linens, the blankets and flannel sheets turned back invitingly. Cade dropped his duffel on the seat of a straight-backed wooden chair, unzipping the bag to pull out clean shorts and a T-shirt. He carried them across the hall and into the bathroom. Here, too, all was neat with clean towels and washcloths hung on the bar next to the sink and shower stall.

Cade stripped and stepped into the shower, letting the hot water pour over him, easing muscles that ached after the long hours he'd spent driving. He'd been on the road by 3:00 a.m. each day, taking advantage of the early morning hours and nearly traffic-free highways.

Toweling off, he slid into his shorts and shirt then went back to the bedroom. Climbing between clean sheets, he fell asleep within moments. Unfortunately, falling asleep loosened his control and memories surfaced once more. He dreamed in vivid, brilliant Technicolor and painful detail.

He was ten years old and his mother, Melanie Coulter, had won the National Arts Award for her copper and silver sculptures. He'd flown to New York City with his parents and brothers for the ceremony, his mother glowing with delight as she walked across the stage. Holding the golden statuette in her hands, she told the crowd that her inspiration came from her husband and four sons, whom she adored. Seated in the front row, Cade looked up to see the pride on his father's face, feel the love and affection in the touch of his big hand on his shoulder. Cade couldn't imagine ever being sad.

The dreamscape changed, flashing forward two years. Swimming in the creek, Cade and his brothers teased their mother, coaxing her to join them. They'd all swung on the rope over the creek hundreds of times, but this time it broke and Melanie fell, hitting her head on a rock.

In Cade's dream, it happened in slow motion. And as always, he couldn't reach her in time. The dark house, graveside service, grief and muffled sobs were followed by the sharp pain of a broken arm.

The phantom pain was so acute that Cade woke, jack-knifing upright in bed.

His heart pounded in his chest and he scrubbed his hands over his face.

"Just a dream," he muttered aloud. He absently rubbed his bicep where the injury had long since healed.

The upper arm bone was broken when he'd stepped between his father and younger brother Eli during one of Joseph's drunken rages. It wasn't the first nor the only time he'd deflected his father's anger to keep him from hitting one of his younger brothers. Cade had never understood why his father blamed his sons for their mother's death. He only knew Joseph had plunged them all into a hellish existence when he started drinking the day they buried their mother.

And he still didn't know, he thought grimly. And even if Joseph had known the answer, he no longer could explain.

Cade stretched out on the mattress and closed his eyes, willing himself to rest undisturbed. This time, his exhausted body took over and he fell into deep, dream-less sleep.

Mariah left for work at the Indian Springs Café before daylight the next morning; the moon rode low on the horizon and stars still glittered in the dark sky. The bunkhouse was dark but lamplight gleamed from the ranch house kitchen and living room windows.

Clearly, Cade Coulter was an early riser. She wondered how he'd spent his first night back in his child-hood home after being absent for so many years. Had he felt like a stranger or had he felt welcomed by the old house? She'd grown up in a suburban rambler in a small town in Colorado. Her parents were older when she was born and sadly, she'd lost both of them before she was a senior in college. The house had to be sold to pay her mother's medical bills. Any remnants of home were long gone.

Mariah couldn't imagine purposely staying away from her father and a home like the Triple C for long years.

She parked down the street from the brightly lit windows of the Indian Springs Café. Shivering, she left her car, tucking her chin into her muffler and hurrying down the sidewalk. When she pushed open the café door, warmth engulfed her and she sighed with relief.

"Hi, Mariah." Ed, husband of the café owner, Sally McKinstry, grinned at her, his deep voice booming. "Cold enough for you?"

"Too cold. When's it going to be spring?" Mariah demanded, shrugging out of her jacket and unwinding her gray knit muffler from her throat. She tugged off the matching hat as she crossed the café to the kitchen entry. One end of the kitchen had a door that led into a small utility room where the walls were ringed with hooks. Mariah hung up her outer things, slipped her purse into a small employee's locker and spun the dial. She took a clean white apron from the stack just inside the door and walked back into the kitchen, tying the apron strings around her waist as she moved.

Ed was just removing a tray of homemade cinnamon rolls from the oven and Mariah drew a deep breath, closing her eyes at the mouthwatering scent.

"Ed, I swear, if you weren't already married, I'd

propose if you'd promise to bake me cinnamon rolls every morning," she told him.

He laughed, a deep merry chuckle that echoed in the room. "I'm afraid Sally would skin me alive if I took you up on that."

Mariah took a tray of frosted rolls from his big hands. "Just my luck." She winked and left the kitchen to join Sally behind the long counter.

"Were you flirting with my husband?" Sally asked her with a smile.

"Only because of his cinnamon rolls." Mariah slid the tray of rolls inside the glass counter case, already nearly filled with fresh pies, cakes and Ed's famous chocolate-caramel bars. "You were so smart to marry a man who can bake, Sally."

"You've got that right." Sally nodded emphatically, her blue eyes twinkling behind wire-framed glasses. "A husband who can cook is worth his weight in gold."

Mariah had a swift image of Ed's big frame and solid muscles. "I can't afford him," she determined. "But that doesn't mean I don't appreciate his bakery items," she assured Sally.

"Lucky for you free meals are a perk of your job," Sally told her.

The outer door opened, the string of bells hanging from the handle jingling merrily, and a tall brunette burst into the room. "Morning, you two." She shed her coat as she skirted the tables to disappear through the kitchen door. "Hi, Ed." Her cheery hello was followed by a rumbled greeting from the baker and then she re-entered the dining area. "How's everything with you guys this morning?"

"Fine, Julie. How about you?" Mariah picked up a

box of salt and one of pepper and headed for the table nearest the door.

"Bob took me to a movie last night—the new thriller with Leanne Crystal."

"How was it?" Mariah finished filling the salt and pepper shakers and moved to the next table.

Julie shrugged and picked up the pepper shaker. "All right, I guess. I thought the heroine took silly risks—all to make the hero look as if he was saving the day."

"I hate movies like that," Mariah commented.

"Yeah," Julie agreed. "Give me a romantic comedy any day." She paused abruptly, half-filled pepper shaker in hand. "Hey, I just remembered—we ran into Linda Barnes at the theater. You know her, right? She's Ned Anderson's legal secretary and she told me one of the Coulter boys is back in town. Have you seen him?"

"Yes." Mariah nodded, screwing the shiny metal lid back onto the glass salt shaker.

"Which one is he?"

"Joseph's oldest son, Cade."

"Linda said he's incredibly good-looking, but kind of scary."

"Scary?" Mariah frowned, considering. "I think he seems a little edgy."

"Did he tell you where he's been all these years?" Julie asked, blatantly curious.

"He said he was working in Mexico just before coming home but that's all I know."

"I wonder where his brothers are? Have you heard from any of them?"

"No, I haven't. Although maybe Cade knows more about them."

"Well, I hope they show up soon," Julie said. "Bob

told me the taxes on the Triple C must be humungous and the sooner the heirs talk to the IRS, the better chance they have to work out a deal."

Since Julie's husband was an accountant, Mariah assumed he'd had experience with the IRS and probably was right.

She wiped spilled grains of salt off the wood tabletop.

"I hope they're found soon, too." Mariah picked up the box of salt and moved to the next table. "Joseph wanted them to return and live on the Triple C. He'd be terribly disappointed if they can't all be found."

The growl of powerful engines sounded in the street outside and headlights swept over the front of the café. Mariah glanced out the big plate glass window at six men piling out of two dual-wheeled pickup trucks.

"Sally," she said over her shoulder. "Here come the Turner boys."

Sally looked up, pausing at the far end of the counter where she was stacking clean pottery mugs on a tray next to the big coffeemaker. "Ed," she called into the kitchen. "The Turners just drove up."

"Gotcha." Ed's rumbled response was followed by the sizzle of bacon being dropped on the hot grill. The Turners ate breakfast every morning at the café and always ordered a pound of bacon and two dozen scrambled eggs. Nobody bothered counting the number of refills on coffee—instead, Mariah delivered two filled carafes to their table and replaced them when they were emptied.

The arrival of the six brothers who owned the Double Bar T ranch several miles out of town began the breakfast rush. Mariah quickly became too busy to ponder the enigma that was Cade Coulter.

Cade spent the early morning hours going over the ranch's books. The oak lawyer's bookcase in the corner of the office held hardback ledgers that dated back to the late 1800s when the ranch was built. Fortunately, he didn't need to review all the ledgers. He gave the last five years a careful inspection before briefly scanning the entries from the prior twenty years. The evidence was clear—income generated by the once-prosperous ranch had undergone a steep decline the year his mother died. The past five years showed a more gradual decline but nonetheless, it was clear that Joseph Coulter had been holding on by his financial fingertips when illness struck and wiped out his meager bank account.

It was also clear that someone had been buying groceries and making payments on the feed bill in the months since his death.

Since Mariah was the only person on the Triple C with employment away from the ranch, Cade guessed she must have been using her salary to keep the Coulter Cattle Company afloat.

And damn if that didn't stick in his craw.

He slammed the last ledger shut and rose from the desk to return the book to its slot on the shelf.

He strode down the hall, pausing to take his jacket and hat from the hooks by the door. As he stepped off the porch, Pete exited the machine shop, lifting a hand to catch his attention.

"Hey, boss," the older man called as he walked toward Cade.

"Morning, Pete." Cade stopped next to his truck, waiting for the ranchhand to join him.

"Are you headin' into town?" Pete asked as he neared.

"Yeah." Cade eyed the greasy metal gear in Pete's hand. "I want to stop at Miller's Feed Store and talk to them about the bill. Do you need something picked up?"

"Yep." Pete's hands were smeared with black oil where he gripped the metal cogs. "I called the store in town and they told me they have a replacement part for this cracked gear. If we can afford it, of course," he added hastily. "It's for the hay baler. I know we won't be needin' the baler until summer but if I wait until then to work on it, more than likely we won't have it running when we need it."

"Summers were always busy on the Triple C—and Dad kept us working all winter and spring repairing equipment," Cade agreed. "I'll pick up the part. I noticed the ranch books have an account page for Conners Parts store on Main Street. Is that who you called?"

"That's the place." Pete nodded. "Andy Conners retired a few years back and his son-in-law runs it now," he added.

"I went to school with a Kathy Conners," Cade remembered.

"That's Conners's girl. She's married and her husband is running the store now."

Cade shook his head. "Sounds like a lot of things have changed while I've been gone."

Pete shrugged, his blue eyes shrewd. "Time moves on, boss. Nothin' ever stays the same—men get older and the kids take over."

"I guess." Cade pulled open the truck door. "I have a couple of things to see to in town but I should be back with the part in a couple of hours."

"Sounds good." Pete waved a greasy hand at the barn. "I'll start workin' on the backhoe's brakes while you're gone."

"Dad still has the backhoe?" Cade was surprised his dad hadn't sold the valuable piece of equipment to raise cash.

Pete nodded. "It still runs okay but the brakes are pretty much gone."

"You need any parts for it?"

"I won't know till I get it apart," Pete replied. "Only thing I know for sure is that it needs some work. Probably a lot of work. Most things around here do," he ended without rancor.

Cade swept a quick glance over the ranch yard. "Yeah," he said drily. "I guess they do."

"Things are bound to get better." Pete's gaze followed Cade's before he looked back with a firm nod. "Now that you're home, we'll be able to get the Triple C back up and running the way it was before Joseph took sick. And when your brothers are found, there'll be more men to share the work."

"Yeah." Cade doubted whether things would work out quite as smoothly as the old ranch hand expected. He didn't want to comment, though, until he heard from his brothers. He stepped inside the truck. "I only have the two stops at Conners Parts and Miller's Feed, so I should be back in a couple of hours or less."

"See ya, boss." Pete turned, lifting a hand in farewell as he ambled away across the gravel ranch yard while Cade drove off down the lane toward the highway.

It was just after ten o'clock when Cade reached Indian Springs. He'd been focused on reaching the attorney's office before closing time when he'd visited the town yesterday, but this morning he had time to drive slower and notice his surroundings. At first glance, the small ranching town seemed little different than when he and his brothers had left, years ago. On closer inspection, however, Cade noticed new shops tucked in among the old ones.

He parked on Main Street and went into the parts store. Fifteen minutes later, he dropped the new part on the floor of the truck cab and crossed the street to Miller's Feed Store.

He stepped inside and was immediately awash in memories. One of his best friends during school had been Archie Miller, the son of the feed store owner. They'd spent hours hanging out and helping Archie's father in the store. He'd paid them with ice cold soda on hot summer days and hot chocolate and burgers in the winter. The old building was redolent with the scents of hay, leather and an indefinable mix of aromas from sweet molasses grain and chicken feed. Fans turned lazily, suspended from beams below the high ceiling to push warm air back down into the store. The scuffed wooden floors creaked as Cade strode along the aisle to reach the central counter in the back. The scarred wide wood counter hadn't changed, nor had the early 1900s cash register that sat on top of it. But next to the cash register sat a laptop computer hooked up to a printer and fax machine.

Apparently even Indian Springs was connected to the Internet, he thought with amusement. He half turned, scanning what he could see of the store's interior but it seemed he was alone.

"Thanks, Charlie. See you next week." The deep voice sounded from the rear of the store.

Cade looked down an aisle stacked high with bags of feed just in time to see the back door close behind a blocky man.

"Be right with you, mister," he called, taking off a fleece-lined suede vest as he walked toward Cade. "What can I…" He halted abruptly, a wide smile breaking over his features. "Well, I'll be damned. Cade Coulter, you son of a gun. I heard you were back in town." He strode quickly forward, holding out his hand.

"Hello, Archie." Cade clasped his friend's hand, then thumbed back his Stetson and grinned at him. "I didn't expect to see you here. The last I heard before I left town was that you'd married a girl from Helena and settled there."

"I did," Archie agreed, a shadow dimming his smile. "But she died giving birth to our little girl."

"Damn." Cade's smile disappeared. "I'm sorry to hear that."

"Yeah, well…" Archie shrugged. "It was five years ago. Life goes on." He waved a hand, the gesture indicating the aisles of the store. "Dad has a bad heart and his health was declining—he needed me here so I packed up Kayla and came home. Been here ever since."

"How's your dad doing?"

"Better since he stepped back to working part-time. He and Mom take care of Kayla while I run the store—it works out for all of us."

"Sounds like your parents are lucky to have you—and you're lucky to have them," Cade said.

Archie nodded, his expression somber. "I heard about your dad passing," Archie told him.

"We weren't exactly on speaking terms when I left town." Cade shoved his hands in his jacket pockets. He and Archie had been friends in high school and knew each other's fathers well. "That never changed."

"I heard," Archie said. "Also heard the estate attorney was looking for you and your brothers. Where'd he find you?"

"Mexico."

"No kidding?" Archie's eyes were curious. "What were you doing down there?"

"Working on a ranch."

"I thought you went into the military when you left town?"

"I did." Cade nodded. "I was shot up overseas a few years ago and when they offered me a desk job, I left. Sitting inside an office isn't how I want to spend my life."

"I know what you mean. If all I did here was paperwork, I'd have to leave." Archie's gaze flicked over the high-ceilinged building filled with the scents of hay and leather before returning to Cade. "What about your brothers? Have you heard from them?"

Cade shrugged. "I haven't talked to them yet but I'm sure it's just a matter of time."

"That's good." Archie slapped Cade on the shoulder. "I bet the crew on the Triple C is glad you're back."

"Pete's an old hand so I'm guessing he's glad to have an owner willing to take over the place. But as for the kid and the blonde..." Cade grimaced. "I'm not so sure."

"J. T. Butler's been in and out of trouble since he was

in kindergarten," Archie commented. "Seems to have settled down since he landed out at the Triple C, so I'm guessing he's happy to have one of you Coulters here to keep the place running. And Mariah..." Archie's face softened. "Well, I can't see Mariah Jones being anything other than downright happy to have one of Joseph's sons home."

His comment reminded Cade that he'd planned to ask about those payments on the feed store account recorded in the ledger. "I assume she's the one that's been making token payments on the ranch's feed bill?"

Archie nodded. "I told her she didn't have to because the estate would pay, sooner or later. But she was determined, said Joseph hated being in debt, so I took her money."

"The Triple C account is actually why I stopped in. I went over the books this morning. I'd like to pay off the line of credit you've been running for the ranch."

"I'm always happy to take money, Cade. But your family has a long history with the store and if you need to get feed on credit in the future, just let me know."

"Thanks, Archie. I appreciate it." Cade took his wallet from his back pocket, waiting while Archie pulled up a file on the laptop and hit print.

When he left the feed store some ten minutes later, Cade's bank account was lighter and Archie had wrung a promise from him to stop by the house and say hello to his parents.

His stomach growled and Cade glanced at his watch, realizing he'd last eaten dry toast and coffee at four o'clock. That was seven hours ago.

He glanced down the street. A sign swung above a building a block away, declaring the Indian Springs Café was open for business. Cade strode down the sidewalk, noting with curiosity the businesses lining the downtown blocks of Main Street. Surprisingly, he recognized quite a few of them.

He pushed open the door to the café and stepped inside, pausing to scan the interior. Damn. His quick survey didn't find the silvery sheen of Mariah's blond hair. The anticipation that had buoyed him and quickened his steps instantly deflated, replaced by a sharp twist of disappointment. His stomach rumbled at the aromas of fresh coffee, cinnamon rolls and hamburgers fresh off the grill, reminding him just how hungry he was and he searched the room with another quick glance, spotting an empty booth near the back of the big room. He'd barely had time to hang his coat and hat on the hook and slide into the seat before a dark-haired waitress appeared.

"Good morning," she said cheerfully, setting a glass of water in front of him and handing him a plastic-backed menu. "Your waitress will be with you soon." She lifted a glass carafe of coffee. "Coffee?"

"Yeah, please."

She grinned at him, quickly and efficiently filling his mug before whisking away to refill other customers' cups.

Cade glanced at the menu and set it aside. He leaned back in the booth, scanning the restaurant over the rim of his coffee mug. A middle-aged woman wearing an apron, white shirt and jeans, a pencil tucked into the blond curls above one ear, stood behind the counter. Facing her, three men dressed in battered cowboy hats, faded jeans and boots were seated on the round, blue-vinyl-covered seats of chrome stools, carrying on what seemed to be a good-natured argument.

"I'm telling you, Sally, Mason Turner is the best bull rider in Indian Springs. In fact," the elderly cowboy continued, "I'd bet money he'll beat everybody at the county fair rodeo this summer."

"Nah," the cowboy on his right hooted with derision. "Mason Turner can't hold a candle to that youngest boy of Jack McConnell's. Now that kid can stick on the back of a bull like he was glued there."

"The McConnell kid is pretty good, Asa," the third cowboy put in. "Not sayin' he can beat Turner," he added hastily when the first cowboy turned on him with a ferocious frown. "But he's pretty good."

Cade hid a smile. Asa Kelly had been a friend of his parents, as had the other two older men, Wayne Smalley and Ben Holcomb. The three had been friends since they were kids and were fixtures in Indian Springs, having lived there all their lives.

"What do you think, Mariah?" Asa demanded.

"Oh, no you don't." The feminine voice was underlaid with amusement. "I'm not taking sides—especially since I don't have a clue what you're talking about."

Cade's muscles tensed. He knew that voice, felt its sensual stroke over his skin, and all his senses came alive. He turned his head in time to see Mariah, just inside the door swinging closed at the far end of the counter. She carried a tray loaded with glasses and moved behind the lunch counter to set the tray next to a big coffee urn. The blond waitress murmured to her and she glanced over her shoulder, her brown eyes flaring with awareness as her gaze met Cade's. Then she turned back to quickly unload the glasses from the tray onto the counter.

A moment later, she walked toward him, skirting the tables that filled the space between the booths lining the walls on two sides.

Cade watched her draw near, aware that he was staring but unable, and unwilling, to look away. She was strikingly beautiful and yet seemed unaware of men's glances that followed her passing. It was easy to see why his father had hired her to work on the Triple C and then left her a valuable piece of the ranch, he thought cynically. Mariah Jones's pretty face and curvy body were enough to tempt any man—and Joseph had lived alone for a long time.

"Good morning, boss," she said, pencil poised above a pad, her musical voice polite and carefully neutral. "What can I get you?"

"Morning," he responded. Her lashes lowered, fanning in dark crescents against her fair skin as she glanced down at her pad. Cade waited until she looked up again and when she did, he knew a flare of satisfaction at the turbulence in her dark eyes. Knowing he wasn't the only one caught in the web of sensual attraction that spun between them somehow eased the restlessness that rode him. "I'll have a cheeseburger with everything."

"Anything to drink besides coffee?" She jotted a note and paused to glance up at him.

"No, thanks."

She nodded and moved quickly to the next booth, where a young couple with a toddler were shedding coats and settling in. Cade's gaze followed the slight sway of her hips.

"Well, I'll be damned."

Cade looked over his shoulder. Asa limped toward him, a broad smile wreathing his weathered face. Wayne and Ben were right behind him, their eyes bright with delight.

"Asa." Cade stood, taking Asa's gnarled hand in his. Despite his age, Asa's grip was firm and strong. "Ben, Wayne." He shook their hands, as well. "It's good to see you."

"Where the hell have you been, boy?" Asa demanded. "I was starting to wonder if you'd been killed."

"Nah," Cade said with a grin. "I'm too mean to die."

Ben snorted. "You've been saying that since you were five years old and broke your arm when you fell off the barn roof. I still don't believe it."

"I heard you joined the Marines and went overseas, Cade. Is that where the attorney found you?" Wayne's shrewd blue gaze scanned Cade's features.

"I was in the Marine Corps and spent a lot of time overseas during the last ten years," Cade confirmed. "But I've been a civilian for a while and was working in Mexico when I got the letter from Ned Anderson." He gestured at the bench opposite him. "Can I buy you all a cup of coffee?"

"Sure." Asa slid onto the seat with Wayne while Ben pulled up a chair from a nearby table.

"Hey, Mariah." Ben caught her attention as she turned from the young couple. "Can we have our coffee over here?"

"Sure." She gave him an affectionate smile.

Cade couldn't help but register the difference between the warmth in her voice as she answered Ben and the polite but reserved tone she'd used earlier with him. He didn't like it. And even acknowledging that he cared one way or the other was unusual enough to make him uncomfortable. He'd had good-looking women working for him in the past and he'd never cared whether or not they liked him.

"How are things out at the Triple C?" Wayne asked.

"I haven't had a chance to check things out in any detail," Cade told him. "I've only been here since yesterday—but my first impression is that it needs a lot of work."

"I'm not surprised." Wayne nodded sagely. "We haven't been out there in years. Your dad pretty much turned into a hermit when you boys left. About a week after you were gone, he ran us off with a shotgun when we tried to check on him. We hated doing it but we stayed away since then." Wayne's face turned somber. "Then we heard he stopped drinking over the last years and we drove out to the ranch but couldn't get past the porch. He never asked us inside the house."

"Yeah," Ben agreed, shaking his head. "He wasn't the same Joseph we'd known for so long."

"He changed after Mom died," Cade said noncommittally. "I'm surprised to hear he stopped drinking."

"Too damn bad he didn't stop hitting the bottle before you boys left," Asa said bluntly. "Maybe you wouldn't have gone."

Cade shrugged. "Maybe."

"What are your brothers doing?" Asa asked, his voice curious.

"I'm not sure what they're up to right now," Cade said. "I haven't talked to any of them for several months."

"They travelin' around, are they?" Ben asked, his dark eyes curious.

"None of us have spent a lot of time in one place since we left Indian Springs," Cade confirmed. "Zach works out of an office in San Francisco but he's rarely there so we stay in touch by cell phone."

"What about Brodie and Eli?" Wayne queried.

"Brodie's always moved around, following the rodeo circuit. Last I heard from Eli, he was in Santa Fe."

"Are they on their way home to Montana?" Asa asked.

"Not as far as I know."

"You mean you don't know where they are now?" Wayne put in, surprise coloring his cigarette-gravelly voice.

"Nope." Cade rarely talked about his brothers but the curiosity on the three weathered faces, coupled with their obvious expectation that he'd fill them in and their longtime friendship with his mother, compelled him into speech. "No one's answering their cell phones. I've left messages asking them to call as soon as they can but so far, no replies."

"Well, I'll be damned." Asa shook his head. "Never heard of a family that couldn't get in touch when something happened to one of them."

Mariah, clearing a recently vacated table only a few feet away, glanced up in time to see the slow smile that curved Cade's mouth and spread to his eyes. Amusement turned his stern face from handsome to irresistible. Her breath caught.

"Hell, Asa," Cade drawled. "Our mother was Melanie Coulter. What made you think any of us would do what normal families do?"

Asa laughed, a deep chuckle of amusement. "You're

right, boy. Melanie would be rolling her eyes and laughing at me if she were here."

Mariah tarried at the nearby table as long as she could, fascinated by the interaction between Cade and the three old cowboys. The four clearly shared a history, and just as clearly, a deep affection ran between them, strong and sure despite their long separation.

Reluctantly, she finished clearing the table and moved on to the next, disappointed that she could no longer hear the conversation between the four. A burst of laughter came from the booth and she glanced over her shoulder. The four lounged easily in their seats, laughing as Asa waved his hands in emphasis as he talked.

Ten minutes later, she neared the booth once more to set a hot plate holding a cheeseburger and french fries on the table in front of Cade.

"More coffee?" she asked all four men, receiving nods of confirmation.

"What time do you finish here today?" Cade asked as she poured coffee into his nearly empty mug.

She glanced at her watch. "Sally needs me to stay till one-thirty." She steeled herself for the slam of attraction that hit her each time her eyes met his and looked back at him. Faint lines radiated from the corners of his eyes, paler against the tanned skin and testimony to long hours spent outside, squinting against the sun's rays. His lips were relaxed, slightly curved in a half smile as if still amused at Asa. Mariah couldn't help but wonder what it would be like to be kissed by Cade. A faint shiver at the thought shook her, making her realize she hadn't really answered his earlier question. "I should be home by two o'clock. Will that work for you?"

He nodded. "I'll either be at the house or down at the machine shop with Pete."

"I suppose he's working on the hay baler—he mentioned it last night before dinner."

"Yes—that and the backhoe. He said it needs brakes."

"Are you helping him repair it?" she asked, curious.

"I'm a fair mechanic," he said, answering what he guessed was her unvoiced question. "If you knew Joseph well, you know he could take an engine apart and put it back together blindfolded. He insisted all of his sons do the same."

A small, affectionate smile curved her mouth. "I knew Joseph was an amazing mechanic, but I hadn't heard his sons were, as well. That's sure to come in handy."

"If the equipment is as run-down as what I've seen so far of the rest of the Triple C, I'm sure it will," he said drily.

Her smile faded. "Yes, well…Joseph was ill for some time. None of us could keep up with all the maintenance the Triple C needs."

"I doubt even Joseph expected a crew of three to stay up with all the work necessary to keep the place in order," he told her.

"Perhaps not," she agreed, the coolness returning to her voice.

"Mariah—order up," someone called.

"I have to go—I'll be ready to go over the books with you at two." She turned, moving quickly.

Cade's gaze followed her as she skirted the tables

to collect a tray of food from the pass-through window into the kitchen, located behind the counter.

"She's a good woman, Cade. She took care of Joseph when he fell sick. Pete and J.T. helped, but Mariah's the one the hospice nurse worked with." Asa's voice was quiet, but Cade caught the warning edge.

"Yeah?" Cade's gaze noted the solemn, confirming nods from Ben and Wayne. "How long did she know him?" He was curious and although he was skeptical of all things connected to Joseph Coulter, he trusted these three men to be truthful.

"About four years, give or take," Ben said. "Summertime, I think it was. She was driving through the county, got sick and passed out, ran her car into the ditch on the highway just past the Triple C arch. Pete found her and took her to the main house. After she was better, she got a job at the café and she's been here ever since."

"Living out at the Triple C?" Cade found it hard to believe his father had let her stay on the ranch when Asa had said earlier that Joseph had avoided them and nearly become a hermit.

"Not at first," Asa told him. "She had an apartment here in town, over on Elm Street. But the building burned down a year later and that's when Joseph offered her housing out at the ranch."

"I see." Cade didn't see, not really, but he let it slide.

The burger was the best he'd had since returning to the States from Mexico. Cade demolished it with remarkable speed while listening as the three old cowboys related the highlights of events in Indian Springs over the last thirteen years. They lingered over coffee until

Cade glanced at his watch and realized it was growing late.

"Much as I hate to, I'd better get going," he said.

Asa nodded. "It's gonna take a while to get a handle on the situation at the Triple C," he said with surety. "Let us know if we can do anything. In fact…" his face brightened. "Maybe we'll just head out your way for a visit later this week."

"Sounds good. I look forward to it." Cade shook hands all around and left the booth, pausing at the register just inside the door to the street.

The older blonde he'd seen behind the counter earlier was manning the register. The blue-and-white letters on the name tag clipped to her shirt pocket spelled out her name—Sally.

"You're Joseph Coulter's son, aren't you."

It wasn't a question. Cade guessed the news of his return had been passed along the gossip grapevine at the speed of light. More than likely, most of the residents of Indian Springs knew he'd returned.

"I am," he said calmly, handing her the café check and a twenty dollar bill. "Did you know Joseph?" The question was purely to distract her from asking any personal questions.

"Oh, yes. He came in for lunch at least once a week, sometimes more often." She rang up his bill and counted out change. "Not that I can say I knew him well—he was pretty quiet, kept to himself, you know." She leaned a bit closer over the glass-topped counter. "Except for Mariah. Those two were as close as father and daughter. I don't know what he would have done without her when he got sick." She dropped the change due in his hand. "I hope you and your brothers will look out for her, just like your dad did. She doesn't have any other family, you know. In fact, I suspect that's why she and Joseph were so close."

"I appreciate her kindness to our family, ma'am. And I'm sure my brothers and I will return it in kind." He touched the brim of his hat in farewell, shoving the cash into his jeans pocket as he left the café.

He hadn't lied, he thought. Not exactly. If the woman interpreted his reply to mean he planned to indulge Mariah Jones, so what? It seemed clear Mariah was well-liked and firmly entrenched in the Indian Springs community. He wasn't convinced the beautiful blonde didn't have an ulterior motive in cultivating Joseph's friendship, but clearly the situation merited further investigation.

The prospect of "investigating" Mariah was too damned appealing, he thought. He needed to focus on the Triple C and its problems—not on Mariah Jones.

Chapter Four

Mariah watched surreptitiously as Sally rang up Cade's tab before he left the café, the door closing firmly behind his tall, broad-shouldered form. A moment later, he strode past the large plate glass windows and then disappeared from sight.

She realized she'd been holding her breath, staring after him, and quickly turned back to stuffing napkins into a dispenser.

She had to stop being fascinated by Cade Coulter. He clearly suspected she'd somehow tricked Joseph into leaving her the cabin.

The man thinks you're unethical and a liar, she told herself sternly. *How are you going to convince him he's wrong? There's zero possibility he's going to change his mind.*

Which meant she would never know what it felt like

to kiss him. Disappointment, unwelcome and unwanted, followed the thought and Mariah frowned, cramming napkins into an empty dispenser with unnecessary force.

Not for the first time, she wished Joseph was still here—then he could deal with his son.

She wondered what the other three Coulter brothers were like. If they were all as unyielding as Cade, she wasn't sure she was ready to deal with four of them coming home.

She finished her shift early and returned home in time for a quick shower, pulling on jeans and a warm sweater before heading back outside. It was just before two o'clock when she walked from her house to the main buildings. Cade's big truck was parked outside the machine shop and she angled toward it, going through the smaller door to reach the interior.

The tap of hammer on metal rang in the building, the deep murmur of male voices reaching her as she stepped inside, the space redolent with the smell of machine oil. A fire roared in the squat black stove in one corner and Mariah unzipped her coat. Pete and Cade were in their shirtsleeves, hands black with grease as they worked on the hay baler. Tools and metal parts lay scattered on the counter behind them.

"Hello," she called as she walked toward them.

"Hey, Mariah," Pete responded as both men looked up and saw her. "When did you get home?"

"Not long ago." She gestured at the equipment they worked on. "How's it going?"

"We're done," Cade said, wiping his hands on a towel already black with grease. "It'll take me a few minutes to put tools away and scrub. Why don't you go on up to the house and I'll be there as soon as I'm finished."

"All right." Mariah retraced her steps, pausing in the doorway to look back. "It's your turn to cook tonight, Pete—can I swap turns with you? I need to be off tomorrow."

"Sure," the older man responded with alacrity. "Got a hot date tomorrow night?"

"Of course." She laughed at the surprise that flashed across his features. "With my book club," she explained with a grin. "It's our monthly dinner meeting." She waggled her fingers at him and went outside.

She'd been inside the main ranch house dozens, if not hundreds, of times over the last four years but as she stepped over the threshold, she realized that this time was different.

Frowning, she glanced around but saw no obvious changes. There was no visible evidence of Cade's presence, not even the magazines on the coffee table seemed disturbed. Nevertheless, she thought, something was different.

The faint aroma of coffee grew stronger as she reached the office. Dropping her coat on the scarred leather sofa, she took a seat in one of the chairs facing the desk.

The living room had been void of signs of Cade's presence, but the office was filled with him. The current year's ledger that she'd left carefully centered on the desktop now topped a stack of similar hardback account books on one side. A sleek, silver laptop computer was in its place, a small pile of what looked like legal documents lying beside it. A coffee mug rested on the other side of the computer, together with a folded newspaper.

She breathed deeply, drawing in the scents in the room.

This is what's different, she realized abruptly. The subtle scent of Cade's aftershave, mingled with the aroma of brewed coffee, tantalized her senses. Cade's presence had chased away the mustiness of a house too long without an occupant. Before Cade's arrival, the house had gradually taken on the chemical smells of medical supplies, prescriptions and disinfectants used during Joseph's illness.

But in one short day, the house had lost its air of waiting and seemed to reflect the energy and leashed power of its new occupant.

Mariah was stunned. If Cade Coulter had this much impact on an inanimate building, what kind of effect would he have on the rest of the Triple C, especially the humans?

Before she could wonder longer, the front door opened and closed, followed by the sound of boots moving down the hallway.

"Sorry to keep you waiting," Cade said as he entered the office. "That took longer than I thought it would."

"Another problem with the hay baler?" she asked, managing to keep her voice calm. If the empty office had felt subtly charged by Cade's energy, his actual presence seemed to shrink the space. Each breath she drew pulled in the faint scent of subtle male aftershave and a slight hint of fresh cold air that seemed to cling to him.

"Just a small one but we fixed it. Pete's moved on to replacing the brakes on the backhoe." He tossed his coat on the end of the sofa next to hers before rounding the desk. He shifted the laptop to one side and settled into the heavy swivel chair. "I have a few questions about some of the entries," he began, taking the top ledger from the stack and flipping it open.

Mariah sat forward, leaning her forearms on the edge of the desk in order to see the page.

"Everything seems fairly clear," he commented. "But I want to verify a few things. There haven't been any withdrawals from the ranch's checking account since Dad died, is that right?"

Mariah nodded. "No one had the authority to write checks on the account."

"But the debit sheet shows the bills have continued to be paid over the last few months." He leaned back in his chair, his gaze narrowed over her. "How were you paying them?"

She was prepared for the blunt question. "I used my salary and tips from my job at the café."

He stared at her for a long moment, his green eyes inscrutable. "Did you tell the estate attorney you were doing this? Did he okay it?"

"I talked to Ned Anderson. He was aware of the immediate cash flow problem we had," Mariah said. "But he told me that he didn't have the power to promise repayment from the estate."

"And yet you spent your own money keeping the Triple C afloat, without a guarantee you'd be repaid?"

"We had to eat and so did the horses and cattle. And the weather was too cold to go without heat so I paid the oil bill. There didn't seem to be a practical alternative." Mariah couldn't tell from Cade's demeanor whether he was glad or angry about using her café salary for the ranch expense. Most people would be grateful, she thought, but she had no idea what Cade Coulter felt. "It's not as if I had a choice. Not one I was aware of, anyway," she added.

His green eyes narrowed, considering her as if weighing her words. Then he nodded slowly, his gaze warming. "I can't see an alternative, either. I appreciate your willingness to step up. My brothers and I owe you for what you've done." He sat forward, took a check from beneath the laptop and handed it to her. "This is for the total amount you paid according to the ledger entries. If you have other receipts not recorded here, get them for me and I'll cut you another check."

Mariah accepted the check without looking at the amount, feeling a heady rush at his warmer, friendlier tone. "Thank you, but I wrote everything in the ledger." She glanced at the slim laptop. "Will you be keeping ranch records on the computer?"

"Eventually," he told her. "I don't have the software program for it but the ranches where I've worked over the last few years all had computerized records, including calf production and pasture rotation."

"I've heard of those programs," she said. "The Turners use one."

"I went to school with Jed Turner and his brothers. I'll have to call him and get the name of the program he's using." He glanced at the stack of ledgers, the pile of correspondence and his laptop. "Just as soon as I have time," he added with a grimace. "A new bookkeeping system isn't on my list of top ten things to make happen. I'm not sure it would even make it into the top twenty."

"Have you heard from your brothers yet?"

"No." He thrust his fingers through his hair, raking back the black strands off his forehead. "I hope they check in soon. There are a lot of decisions to be made and most of them won't be legal without my brothers signing off."

Mariah's heart sank at the confirmation that hard times on the Triple C weren't over yet. "Do you know where they are? The attorney told Pete his office hadn't been able to locate them."

"I have a general idea," Cade said. "Zach's usually the easiest to reach because he works out of an office in San Francisco as a financial analyst, though he's not there very often. But he's not answering his cell phone and neither is his assistant. Brodie's normally not that hard to find, either," he went on. "He follows the rodeo circuit, so once you know his schedule, it might take some time, but he's reachable. Ned said he'd have the investigator start searching." Cade frowned, his gaze distracted. "But Eli... He's the one who drops out of sight every now and then. He doesn't have a permanent address and he can be a tough cat to track."

"How long since you've seen your brothers?" she asked.

Cade shrugged. "I saw Zach a year ago, Brodie less than that and Eli..." He paused, thinking. "I guess it's been a bit over a year since Eli and I were both in Vegas together."

"My goodness." Mariah was beginning to understand that locating the Coulter men wasn't going to prove as easy as she'd hoped. She decided to ask the question that had plagued her ever since Joseph's death.

"I've wanted to ask you," she said, her gaze direct.

"Do you plan to keep Pete, J.T. and myself on? Or will you let us all go when your brothers return?"

Dark brows lifted in surprise. "Why would I lay you off? As far as I can tell, the three of you have managed to keep the ranch from going under for the last few months. And you did it without regular salaries or any guarantee you'd ever get paid. And even with all my brothers here, it takes more than us—plus you three— to keep the Triple C running. It's more likely we'll hire more hands, not let anyone go."

She felt her cheeks warm under his gaze. "I'm glad to hear that. All of us consider the Triple C our home. I don't know where Pete and J.T. would go if they had to leave here."

His expression cooled, his eyes unreadable. "You don't have that concern."

"No." His reference to her having a home in the cabin on the Triple C was clear—and just as clear that he still wasn't pleased by her inheritance from Joseph.

"I'm not sure if you understand the history attached to the cabin my father gave you." The friendly warmth was gone from his voice, though he was polite. "My grandfather built it for my grandmother before they married. It's landlocked, surrounded by Coulter-owned acres. I don't know why my father decided to give you that particular piece of property but doing so creates a hole in the ranch. I'll buy it from you at fair market value, and help you find a comparable house and three acres somewhere else."

She shouldn't have been surprised, Mariah thought, but nonetheless, the feeling he was rejecting her stung. "I'm afraid I can't do that. I promised Joseph I would stay on the Triple C and help you and your brothers when you returned. And," she said quickly when his frown indicated he was about to question her, "I've grown attached to the cabin after living there over the last few years. It's become my home."

"You'll feel the same way about a different place in a few years," he told her.

"No, I don't think so." She searched for the words to make him understand. "When Joseph let me live in the cabin, he gave me more than housing. He made me part of the family here—with him, Pete and J.T.—when I was alone and had no one. I owe him for that."

He leaned forward, his turbulent green eyes pinning her. "If you really feel you owe him, sell me the land. The ranch shouldn't be split up."

"I'm sorry. I can't. And I've read the will. I know the heirs can't challenge the terms of the will without losing their inheritance." His eyes darkened, and his mouth tightened, but before he could argue further, Mariah glanced at her watch and straightened. "Look at the time. I have to get dinner started or we'll be eating too late. If we're done here," she added belatedly.

"Yeah, we're finished." He stood, grabbing up his coat. "I'll walk out with you. I want to check with Pete, see if he needs any help with the backhoe."

Mariah was vividly aware of Cade walking behind her down the hall and out of the house, then beside her as they crossed the ranch yard. Despite her long legs and five foot six inches of height, he loomed over her. Not only was he tall, but he was powerfully built, the sheepskin-lined coat making his chest and shoulders appear even broader.

Unlike the small town she'd grown up in, Indian Springs seemed full of big men, their bodies muscled by heavy ranch work. Cade Coulter, however, also had a presence and aura of danger that made her feel smaller and infinitely feminine. It was almost as if the sheer maleness of him resonated with her on some visceral level.

She'd never before known anyone like him.

She was instinctively wary around him at the same time she was inexorably drawn nearer.

They said goodbye, Cade disappearing into the machine shop while she continued on to the bunkhouse.

A woman needed to be careful around a man like him, she cautioned herself as she climbed the shallow steps to the bunkhouse porch.

Three hours later, Mariah sat at the table, an empty plate in front of her, listening to Cade. J.T. and Pete were kicked back in their chairs but she noticed both of them were tense beneath their seemingly casual posture.

"I spent the afternoon talking to Pete, and Mariah," he added, his green gaze flicking to her in acknowledgment. "I want one of you to go with me tomorrow while I drive around the ranch. I need to get a feel for exactly how much work needs to be done and since you three have been here for the last few years, I'd like your input."

"I'd be glad to skip school and go with you," J.T. said promptly.

"No." Cade's response was instant. "I don't want you missing school for this. It's going to take more than one day. You can go with me on the weekend."

"I'd like to go with you, boss," Pete said with regret, rubbing his palm over his chin. "But I have to go to the doc in Wolf Point."

"What's wrong?" Cade's gaze sharpened.

"Nothin, nothin," Pete said hastily. "I had a little trouble with my heart last year and the doc makes me come back every six months for a checkup, that's all."

Which leaves me, Mariah realized. She met Cade's green gaze. "I can go—I'm not scheduled to work at the café tomorrow. What time do you want to leave?"

"Not too early," he said. "How about eight o'clock?"

She nodded. "That's fine."

"Good." Cade poured more coffee into his mug and settled back, tilting the chair onto its rear legs to lean against the wall. He pinned each of them in turn with a sober stare. "I don't need to tell you three that the Triple C has a lot of problems. I'll have a better handle on exactly where we are after tomorrow but I can't afford to wait until my brothers are here before coming up with a plan." He swept the three of them with a grim glance. "The inheritance taxes on this place are astronomical. I'm not sure how we're going to pay them without selling off acres—which I can't do unless all my brothers agree. Besides, I don't want to use that option unless we have to. Dad left me the cattle and all the other stock, separate from my brothers. I've decided to sell off the steers. We'll comb the pastures for as many cattle as we can find and drive them home. If we're lucky, I'll net enough profit to make the first payment on the taxes."

Mariah's heart lifted with hope. She glanced at Pete and saw him exchanging an equally hopeful look with J.T.

"Even if I didn't plan to sell the steers," Cade continued, "we need to round up stock and count the cattle. From what Pete tells me, Dad hasn't done more than count the cows in the home pastures since Pete's worked here."

"I've been here for seven years," Pete commented. "Joseph and me never rode farther than the south pasture. He said he didn't want to bother with a few strays. I figured he'd brought the main herd home from the outer pastures before I hired on."

"He probably did. But there are a couple of places in the breaks that are impossible to fence because the country's so rough. Granted, it takes a determined cow to climb up and out but it's possible. When we were kids, we'd take gear and pack in, spend a week camping out, long hours hunting and driving two or three dozen head of cattle home."

"I've never been on a roundup," J.T. put in, his gaze intent on Cade. "Sounds like it might be fun."

Mariah suppressed a smile at the anticipation in J.T.'s voice. Normally, the teenager acted far more mature than his seventeen years, rarely exhibiting youthful enthusiasm. It was nice to see the animation in his expression.

Cade snorted. "*Fun* isn't the word I'd use," he said. "Chasing cattle that have been running wild for years is hard, dirty work. By the time we get the herd home, you'll feel like you've been in the saddle for a month and every bone in your body will hurt." A smile curled his mouth at J.T.'s expression. "And that's if it's the middle of the summer and the weather is nice. This is March and it gets damn cold at night. So you'll get little or no sleep and then spend twelve to fifteen hours in the saddle."

"And this time of year," Pete warned, his eyes glinting with humor, "you're likely to get rained or snowed on, hard to tell which. So you'll be cold *and* wet."

"Couldn't we take a truck?" J.T. asked. "With a good heater to use when we get wet and half-frozen?"

Cade chuckled. "A truck wouldn't get far in that rough country. Sometimes even horses have trouble. The best mount is a mule, young and strong, sure-footed and stubborn."

"Are you riding Jiggs?" J.T. asked.

"I always ride Jiggs. He's tireless and nothing fazes him." Cade looked at Pete. "What about you and J.T.? Do you have cow ponies?"

Mariah realized he hadn't included her in the question but before she could comment, Pete replied.

"I have a ten-year-old quarterhorse that's good with cattle. J.T. can ride Joseph's horse, Sarge. The gelding has some age on him but he's solid."

"And I have my own horse, too," Mariah said.

Cade's green gaze sharpened over her. "You're not going," he said flatly.

"Why not?" she bristled.

"Because it's no place for a woman."

"I want to go," she said firmly. "I'm a good rider—just ask Pete."

Cade's gaze flicked to the older man.

"It's true," Pete confirmed. "The girl can ride."

"It's still not a job for a woman," Cade said, his jaw set.

"You said earlier this afternoon that you and your brothers owe me. If you meant that, then treat me the same way you would Pete and J.T. I don't want to stay at home while the rest of the crew is out doing what needs to be done. I want to contribute. I want to hold up my end just like everyone else who works on the Triple C."

Cade's jaw was set so tightly, Mariah was surprised she couldn't hear his teeth grind.

"I'll think about it," he said.

"But I…" she began.

"I said I'll think about it," he said with finality. "I'll see you at eight tomorrow morning. We'll take my truck."

Mariah nodded, unwilling to tell him that she usually indulged herself and slept in until eight o'clock on her days off from the café. The prospect of spending several hours in the close confines of a truck cab with Cade Coulter made her shiver. Whether the reaction was caused by female interest or apprehension, she wasn't quite sure.

Mariah's alarm rang at seven o'clock the following morning. She staggered out of bed and fumbled her way into the kitchen to turn on the coffeemaker. She leaned against the counter, waiting for it to brew so she could carry a steaming mug into the bathroom with her.

At ten minutes to eight, when she left the cabin and headed up the lane toward the ranch house, she was fully awake. She carried a travel mug in one hand and a backpack slung over one shoulder. Since she had no idea how long Cade planned to be gone, she'd packed a substantial lunch that was big enough for two. The food was stored in her backpack, together with a thermos filled with more coffee.

Mariah was a woman who liked being prepared for any eventuality. In the past, life had handed her too many surprises. She'd learned a valuable lesson at the tender age of eight when her mother was diagnosed with kidney disease. Twice a week during summer and other school vacations, she'd packed a bag with bottled water, snacks and books to accompany her mother on hospital visits for dialysis treatments. Ever after, she'd automatically carried a backpack with roughly the same essentials whenever she knew she'd be away from home for several hours.

The Girl Scouts would be proud of me, she thought, leaning against the tailgate of Cade's pickup. She sipped her coffee, her gaze sweeping the quiet yard. Jiggs stood at the corral fence, his ears pricked forward, his intelligent gaze fixed on her.

Mariah grinned and waggled her fingers at him. His ears flicked in response and he bobbed his head.

I'm waving hello to a horse, she thought wryly. *I need to get a life. The only males interested in me are horses.*

A door slammed behind her and she glanced over her shoulder, straightening when she saw Cade loping down the porch steps toward her.

But I'm definitely interested in this male, she thought with an inward sigh. Too bad nothing could ever come of it since she was convinced Cade still suspected she'd somehow taken advantage of Joseph's illness to gain the cabin.

"Good morning," she called as he drew near.

"Morning."

His eyes narrowed, thick black lashes lowering briefly as his gaze swept her with an all encompassing glance.

Mariah steeled herself against the shiver of purely sexual reaction she felt each time he gave her one of those long, heated looks. And he did it every time he saw her, she thought, helpless to stop the flush of arousal that she knew was probably turning her cheeks pink.

Maybe he won't notice, she thought, *or if he does, he'll think I'm just cold.*

"Ready to go?" he asked as he walked past her to the passenger door and pulled it open.

"Yes, absolutely." She walked toward him, swinging the backpack off her shoulder as she went.

Cade snagged the pack from her hand and set it in the backseat of the extended cab before letting her move past him. Mariah was thankful for the vehicle's chrome step because the four-wheel-drive truck sat much higher off the ground than her car. Climbing into the cab, however, put her far too close to Cade as he held the door open for her. She drew a deep breath and pulled in the subtle clean scent of his aftershave mingled with the faint aroma of coffee and crisp morning air. She had a sudden urge to turn, bury her face against the warm column of his throat, slide her arms around his waist and press her body against the long, hard length of him from chest to thigh. She controlled the impulse and resolutely kept her back to him as she slid onto the soft leather seat.

Cade waited until she was settled before he closed the door and rounded the hood of the truck to join her inside the cab.

"Where are we going?" she asked, fastening her seat belt, grateful that he didn't appear to have noticed that moment of hesitation.

"I want to take a look at the home pasture." Cade shifted the big truck into gear and drove out of the yard, down the lane that led away from the cluster of ranch buildings, past her cabin and on to the rolling pastures beyond. "We'll drop off a salt block and check the water pump at the windmill. Pete told me that you were the last one to ride the fence lines, is that right?"

She nodded. "I took Sarge out about ten days ago. I had two days off in a row from the café and rode out both days so I had time to check most of the pasture."

"Did you count cows?"

"Only those I came across—mostly I wanted to make sure the fences were holding. Pete was worried about the posts along the east boundary. He thought they should have been replaced last fall but Joseph told him not to bother." She stared pensively out the windshield. "I think he didn't feel well enough to ride out with Pete but didn't want to admit it."

A moment passed as he appeared to absorb her words. "So he was sick for quite a while." Cade's deep voice broke the small silence.

"He was slowing down for nearly a year before he finally went to the doctor and was diagnosed." Mariah glanced sideways at him but his profile was turned toward her as he drove, his gaze focused on the lane ahead, and she couldn't detect emotion on his features. "He wouldn't let me write to you and tell you that he was ill," she added softly. "He said he didn't have the right."

Cade flicked her an enigmatic glance. "Didn't have the right? What the hell does that mean?"

She shrugged. "I don't know. I asked him what he meant but he only repeated the words."

"Huh."

Mariah couldn't interpret his noncommittal grunt, and the hard cast of his features and the set of his jaw discouraged further questions.

He slowed, braking to a stop and throwing the

transmission into neutral a few feet in front of a metal gate blocking the lane.

Mariah unlatched her seat belt and reached for the door release but he stopped her with a quick gesture.

"I'll get the gate," he told her. "Slide over here and drive the truck through."

He shoved open the door and got out. While he unlocked the gate and pulled it wide, Mariah scooted into the driver's seat to shift the vehicle into gear and drive slowly through the opening. Behind her, Cade closed the gate. By the time he reached the truck cab, Mariah was once again in the passenger seat.

The lane quickly became more of a track than a road and the truck bumped and rocked over the rougher ground as they drove deeper into the pasture. Cade asked her several questions about the pasture conditions in comparison to prior years and much to Mariah's relief, accepted her responses. She hadn't been sure whether he'd listen to her opinions or whether he'd assume she wasn't as knowledgeable as Pete or J.T.

And she wasn't, she thought. Pete had years of experience on the Triple C and before that, on other ranches. Fortunately, Cade kept his questions confined to the knowledge she'd gathered during her weekly rides over the pasture acres.

At noon, they were miles from the bunkhouse kitchen and Mariah was glad she'd packed lunch.

When she stepped out of the cab to stretch her legs, Cade caught her waist and lifted her, seating her on the truck's lowered tailgate. Mariah barely had time to catch her breath before he swung up beside her, the backpack between them.

"What did you bring?" he asked.

Mariah unzipped the backpack. "Sandwiches," she told him, handing him a plastic ziplock bag. She removed another one and dropped it into her lap before pulling out several other plastic bags. "And potato chips, dill pickles, apples and cookies."

He lifted an eyebrow, slanting her a look filled with surprise. "You brought all of that for both of us?"

"Please." She rolled her eyes. "I've been out riding fence with J.T. He's a bottomless pit and he never remembers to bring a lunch—which means he always shares mine. If I didn't bring twice as much food as I can actually eat, I'd starve."

His grin widened, green eyes twinkling. "And you thought I'd be like J.T.?"

She shrugged. "I had no idea. But I've learned it's best to be prepared."

"Good plan," he agreed.

The sandwiches were made of slices of thick ham left over from dinner the night before and the two ate in silence for a moment, sharing the bag of chips and pickles.

"This is really good." He indicated his half-eaten sandwich. "Something about it tastes different—I'm guessing you didn't use plain mustard."

"No, I didn't." Mariah shook her head. "It's one of my mother's recipes—she mixed horseradish with a little dill into mustard for my dad. I always liked it so I still use the mix on sandwiches." She smiled with fond remembrance. "My mom was a great cook—everyone in town wanted her recipes."

"Where do your folks live?" he asked with curiosity.

"They're both gone now but we lived in a small town

outside Denver when I was a kid. They lived there all their lives."

"Do you have sisters? Or brothers?"

Mariah met his gaze and read genuine interest there. "No, I was an only child." She stared at a tall butte in the distance. "My parents were in their mid-forties when I was born. Mom told me they'd given up hoping for children. She passed away when I was still in high school and Dad followed her when I was a junior in college."

She drew a long breath, a small smile curving her mouth. "Mom was insistent that I get a college degree—she had such plans for me. Even though she was gone, she'd instilled her dream in me and I applied at the University of Montana. I had scholarships and Dad helped with expenses. But then he suffered a massive heart attack the winter of my junior year."

"How did you wind up in Indian Springs?" he asked, his strong teeth crunching as he bit into a pickle.

"I took a break from school and my part-time job the summer after dad died." She nodded toward the horizon, beyond which lay the Triple C headquarters. "I was on a road trip, driving a loop around the state when I caught the flu and ran my car into the ditch on the highway only yards from the Triple C arch. Pete found me and took me home and Joseph let me stay for a couple of weeks until I recovered. I needed money to have my car repaired and fortunately, Sally happened to need a waitress. So I went to work at the café and four years later," she explained as she spread her hands, "I'm still here."

"So you never got the degree your mom wanted for you." He eyed her. "What did she want you to be—doctor, lawyer, schoolteacher? Something that makes you a successful waitress?"

She laughed, her brown eyes lit with mirth. "I majored in business and public relations but I never thought I'd use it to work as a waitress. The truth is, however, my classes probably do apply to my work in some ways. I can't afford to go back to school anytime soon, though I probably will some day—but I enjoy my job." She shrugged. "I'm not saying I plan to stay at the café forever, but Ed and Sally are great bosses and I like the other women working there. Most of the customers are regulars from Indian Springs and the surrounding ranches and I've met some wonderful people and made some very good friends. In fact," she mused aloud, "I'd say I've found a home here."

"You don't feel the small town where you grew up is still home?" Cade asked, tipping a bottle of water to drink, his green gaze fastened on her.

"Not really. Dad had to sell the house to pay medical bills after my mom passed away and then he died, too, and there didn't seem to be a reason to go back. So…" Her gaze swept the rolling pasture dotted with sagebrush and the imposing butte rising to tower behind them. "I've stayed here. It's beautiful country."

Cade's gaze followed hers and he nodded. "Yeah, if you're a man and like horses, cattle and don't mind driving a few hours to reach a shopping mall."

"Works for me." She popped a slice of apple in her mouth, chewed and swallowed while he stared at her.

"Most women wouldn't think so," he said finally.

Mariah smiled serenely. "I'm not most women."

He stared at her for a moment. "No," he said at last, his voice deeper, faintly rasping. "You're not." His thick lashes half lowered over green eyes darkened with heat.

His gaze dropped to her mouth, lingered, and she caught her breath. At the base of her throat, her pulse pounded in a heavier, faster beat as tendrils of sexual tension spun a web between them. For a long moment, she thought he would reach for her, press his mouth to hers.

But then the line of his mouth tightened and in an abrupt move, he pushed off the tailgate, his boots hitting the ground with an audible thump.

"It's late," he said abruptly. "We'd better start back if we're going to drop off the salt block and get you home in time for your meeting tonight."

Mariah had forgotten all about her book club dinner. "Of course," she murmured. Before she could jump down, Cade's hands were at her waist and once again, he lifted her with ease. His hands didn't linger and he was careful not to let their bodies brush as he lowered her.

They weren't far from home when the ring of a phone interrupted Willie Nelson's distinctive voice singing the lyrics of "Pancho And Lefty." Cade flicked off the CD player and took a silver cell phone out of the cup holder next to his seat.

He glanced at the caller ID phone number and immediately thumbed the phone's on switch.

"Ned—what's up?" He listened for a moment before speaking again. "I'm away from the house, probably out of signal range. Sorry I missed your calls. Have you heard from Zach?"

Mariah held her breath in hope, unaware that she crossed her fingers.

"Damn." Cade's frown visibly reflected the frustration that throbbed in his voice. "How long?" He listened for several minutes, his frown growing blacker. At last, he growled a goodbye and switched off the phone, tossing it back into the cup holder.

"Bad news?" Mariah asked.

"Not good," he said. "Ned finally located Zach's personal assistant. It seems my brother's climbing Mt. Everest, which is why I haven't been able to reach him."

Mariah felt her eyes widen. "He's climbing Mt. Everest?" she repeated in disbelief.

"Yeah." Cade flicked her a quick glance, a reluctant smile curving his mouth. "Don't look so shocked, Ms. Jones," he said with amusement. "That's what Zach does in his spare time. Since we left Montana, he's been climbing mountains, competing in Iron Man contests, swimming with sharks—you name the challenge, he'll try it. If there's a world record, he'll challenge it."

"I see," she said faintly, thinking that she absolutely did *not* see. "Is that what he does for a living—compete in contests?"

"No, he competes for fun. He's employed by a San Francisco company that buys up companies in financial trouble. Then they send Zach in to decide whether to restore the troubled company to financial health before his company resells it, or break up the company to sell off the assets. He's brilliant at it."

"He sounds like a shark," Mariah said dubiously.

"I'm not sure that's accurate but it's pretty close," Cade agreed.

Mariah returned to the bigger question. "Can't you reach him by satellite hookup? I thought climbers on Mt. Everest were closely monitored by safety teams?"

"That's true for most climbers, but Zach's old-school—and he likes to take risks. He isn't carrying a cell phone, or a computer with a satellite link which means he's essentially out of touch and unreachable until he's back down the mountain."

"Did his assistant have any idea when that might be?"

"She thought it might be a few weeks but with Zach, who knows." Cade's voice was grim. "He told her that she didn't have to return to work for another month at least but she's not sure if he was coming straight back to the States after the climb. He'd mentioned something about stopping to surf the North Shore in Hawaii."

Mariah nearly groaned out loud. "What about your other brothers? Have you located them?"

"No."

"What do they do?" Mariah asked, unable to control her curiosity.

"Brodie's a professional rodeo bull rider—he was all around national champion a couple years ago. Eli's a silversmith and a damned good one. He inherited our mother's talent."

"My goodness," Mariah said faintly. "You're a very exceptional family."

"Eli is," Cade agreed. "The rest of us—well, we're pretty much still doing what we've done since we were kids."

Mariah wasn't so sure—it seemed to her that Joseph Coulter's sons were bigger than life and maybe, just maybe, twice as dangerous. And the more she learned about Cade, the more he intrigued her. Spending time with him also seemed to make the sensual pull she felt even stronger.

She wasn't sure she trusted the strength of that attraction between them.

Chapter Five

That evening, Mariah parked outside the Black Bear Bar & Restaurant in Indian Springs just before six o'clock. It was good she was getting away from Cade and the Triple C for a few hours. She needed to be with women and air filled with estrogen, not high-octane testosterone.

Which pretty much describes Cade Coulter, she thought. High-octane testosterone. Maybe that was why she felt hyperaware of her femininity around him.

She caught up her purse, tucked her copy of Jane Austen's *Pride and Prejudice* into the bag and slid out of her car. Her heels clicked on concrete as she crossed the sidewalk and pulled open the door to the restaurant. A wave of delicious aromas from grilled steak to planked salmon greeted her and she realized she was hungry, starving actually. Waving hello to several customers and waitresses, she crossed the dining room to a semi-secluded alcove in the back where three tables had been pushed together and covered with a white tablecloth.

"Hi, Mariah."

She returned greetings from the five book club members already seated at the table, dropping her purse on a seat next to Julie. Easing out of her coat, she hung it on the back of the chair, took out her book and stashed her purse beneath her chair as she sat.

"How did your meeting with your boss go yesterday?" Julie asked. Mariah had told her she had to hurry home after work at the café to go over the books with Cade.

"Fine—he was nice actually."

"You're so lucky." Julie sighed. "A boss who's nice and gorgeous."

Mariah laughed. "Yes but unlike Ed at the café, Cade can't bake cinnamon rolls."

Sally and her friend, Renee, bustled into the restaurant, reaching the alcove amid a chorus of greetings.

"Let's order," Sally suggested when the two had shed coats and were seated across from Julie and Mariah. "I'm starving."

For the next few moments, the conversation centered around the menu, but finally their orders were given to their waiter and drinks sat before them.

Mariah sipped a glass of white wine, confident that any effects would have worn off before she began the drive home in a few hours.

Across from her, Renee licked a bit of salt from the rim of her glass, sipped her margarita, then made a small sound of satisfaction.

"I've been looking forward to this all day," she said.

"It's so nice to share a table with a group of women instead of men."

Her words rang with heartfelt conviction and the other women laughed. Renee worked as housekeeper for the six Turner brothers and it was universally agreed that she was probably the only woman in Indian Springs, perhaps in all of Montana, who could survive in the all-male household.

"I know exactly what you mean," Mariah said. "In fact, I was thinking on my way in to town that it was going to be so nice to be surrounded by clouds of estrogen instead of testosterone."

Beside her, Julie nearly choked on the wine she'd just sipped. Sally burst out laughing and lifted her stemmed glass.

"Hear, hear," she said, her words echoed around the table amid laughter.

"Speaking of men, I understand one of the Coulter boys came home," Renee said, eyeing Mariah with interest. "Which one?"

"The eldest—Cade." Mariah thought she injected just the right note of bland interest in her answer. She'd been asked the question so many times at the café a day earlier that she'd had more than enough practice.

"Ah, I remember him," Renee said with a nod. "He was a school friend of Jed's." A reminiscent smile curved her lips. "The trouble those two could get in to doesn't bear repeating."

"Oh, come on, Renee," Julie urged, leaning forward. "Tell us."

Mariah badly wanted to hear more, too, but didn't want to appear too interested. Indian Springs was a small town and its residents loved nothing more than to speculate about the unmarried people. She didn't want anyone starting rumors about her and Cade.

Especially when she suspected she was far too interested in him for her own good.

Still, she was glad when Renee gave in to the urgings of Julie and the other women at the table.

"All right, all right," Renee conceded with a laugh. "Jed and Cade were about twenty-one years old that year, I think. Brodie was riding in a rodeo at Wolf Point and carloads of his friends drove over to watch him. Which meant half the young men from Indian Springs, from fifteen to thirty, were there. I think there was drinking involved…."

"No!" The women chorused, rolling their eyes and laughing when they realized they'd all responded with the same amused comment.

"Yes," Renee confirmed. "Anyway—I'm not sure what actually started the fight but Jed later insisted that someone made an insulting comment about Brodie's mother. That was enough to have the Coulter brothers fighting and Jed always said no self-respecting Turner could let them fight alone. The four Coulter boys and the six Turners took on all comers—and they were outnumbered three to one. Rumor has it that Cade and Jed were the last ones standing, back-to-back, bloody, bruised and laughing."

"Did anybody go to jail?" Mariah asked.

"Not that I remember—but they were fighting on the backside of the fairgrounds where the rodeo chutes are and they had to rebuild a few of them." Renee smiled fondly. "Cade and his brothers left town the next year, the day after Eli graduated from high school. Without Cade, Jed settled down. He and his brothers still get involved in throwing punches every now and then but nothing like when they were younger."

"What is it with men and fighting?" Julie asked wonderingly.

"It's a guy thing," Kari Lucas said from the other end of the table. "I don't think women will ever understand it—maybe it's comparable to their inability to understand why we love George Clooney movies."

"You're probably right," Mariah said as philosophical nods of agreement went around the table.

The waiter's arrival interrupted them and they sat back to allow him to slide steaming plates of food on the table in front of them. As they ate, the conversation moved on to a discussion of the many reasons they'd universally loved *Pride and Prejudice.*

It was after nine o'clock before they paid their checks, said good-night and left the table. Mariah lingered just inside the exit, chatting with Julie.

"Come to the movies with Bob and me tomorrow night," Julie coaxed. "It's a romantic comedy and you know you love those."

"I'd love to but I should wait to see what's going on out at the Triple C—just in case I have to…" A crash from the bar next door interrupted her and Mariah's eyes widened. "What on earth was that?"

"I don't know." Julie looked over her shoulder at the closed doors to the bar.

"Let's find out. Come on." Mariah pushed open the swinging doors that separated the restaurant from the bar, Julie following her as she stepped over the threshold.

They stopped abruptly, staring at the scene in front of them, the door swinging shut behind them.

Cade Coulter and Jed Turner stood shoulder-to-shoulder, facing three men in the center of the scuffed wooden floor. Several feet away, two men groaned loudly where they lay on the floor amid broken pieces of a table and several chairs. The three men who were still on their feet were disheveled and bruised, red stains on their faces and shirts.

A tall, ruddy-faced blond cowboy wiped blood from his nose with the back of his forearm. "Hell, Jed," he said with disgust. "Why didn't you tell us your friend is one of the Coulters? I wouldn't have taken offense if I'd known he was a local."

"Don't let that stop you," Cade drawled.

"No, man." A second cowboy held up his hands, palms out. "We have no problem with you using our pool table."

The bartender snorted in exasperation. "It's not your table—it belongs to the bar." He leveled a finger at the three cowboys. "And if you start one more fight in here, I'm going to eighty-six you for life. Now go home and sober up. And take your two friends with you," he yelled after them as they headed for the door.

The three paused to pull up the two prone cowboys off the floor, supporting them as they all staggered to the exit and disappeared outside.

Behind them, Jed looked at Cade and laughed.

"Damn, Jed," Cade said as he visibly relaxed, his fists uncurling and tension easing from his big frame. "That was just like old times."

Jed Turner chuckled, clapping a hand on Cade's shoulder. "Yeah, it was, wasn't it? Brings back some memories."

Cade laughed, turning with Jed to resume their game

at the pool tables several feet behind them. His gaze swept the nearly empty bar, stopping abruptly on the two women just inside the adjoining restaurant door.

All the tension that had just drained away returned full force. Mariah stared at him, her eyes wide and an expression of stunned disbelief on her face.

"Aw, hell," he muttered.

"What?" Jed's gaze followed his. He nodded hello at the two women before looking sideways at Cade. "Is there a problem?"

"No," Cade said shortly, not moving. Damn, she looked good. He'd fantasized about what her long legs would look like out of her faded jeans but reality was even better. She wore a neat little black dress that looked like a long sweater and ended just above her knees. The dress clung to her curves and though it had long sleeves and a high rollover collar that ended just below her chin, it was sexy as hell. Her hair was loose, a silvery fall of pale moonlight silk against the black dress. Belatedly, he realized she had a coat slung over one arm.

He glanced at the other woman and recognized the waitress from the café.

He suddenly realized he was staring and abruptly nodded a greeting, waiting until Mariah nodded back. Then the other woman caught her arm and dragged her back through the door into the restaurant.

"That's one good-looking woman," Jed said with male appreciation.

"Yeah." Cade turned away from the now-empty doorway and stalked to the pool table. Jed joined him and Cade narrowed his eyes, studying his friend's face. "You know her?"

"Sure I know her." Jed picked up his pool cue and

resumed the game, bending over the table to line up a shot. The cue tip hit the six ball with a crack and drove it into the side pocket. Jed unbent, rising to walk around the table while he considered his next shot. "I eat breakfast at the café with my brothers most mornings."

"Is she dating anybody?" Cade kept his voice neutral.

"Mariah? Not that I know of." Jed paused, apparently contemplating an angle, then moved on to another possible shot. "I took her out once but she made it clear she wasn't interested in one-night stands. And you know me." Jed shrugged. "I've got no interest in complications." He bent and set up another shot but this time, the ball just missed the pocket. He stood back, resting the butt of his cue stick on the floor. "If I was interested, though, Mariah would be on my short list. Not only is she easy on the eyes, but I like her."

Cade ignored the surge of relief that Mariah didn't belong to anyone and that Jed hadn't slept with her. He didn't want to think about why it mattered so much. He only knew Jed's voluntary revelation that he hadn't been with Mariah calmed the feral roar of possessiveness that took up residence in his gut.

The image of Cade in the bar was seared on Mariah's memory. She barely registered Julie pulling her out of the Black Bear. They said good-night, ducked into their cars and Mariah drove out of town while Julie drove the few blocks to her house.

If Mariah had been given a test on her conversation with Julie after she'd caught sight of Cade, she would have flunked.

She couldn't focus on anything beyond what he'd

looked like, knees slightly bent, fists half-curled at his sides as he and Jed faced off against those three men. He wore black cowboy boots, faded jeans and a black T-shirt that delineated the heavy muscles layered over his shoulders, chest and the six-pack of his abs. Beneath the short sleeves of the black tee, his biceps flexed with power. The air in the saloon had vibrated with danger and when he'd turned to stare at her, his green eyes were alive with heat and an energy that was electrifying.

If she'd believed she could ignore the attraction she felt for Cade Coulter, she had the feeling she'd been wrong. She'd never met anyone like him before and the possibility that he might feel some of the passion he stirred in her made her shiver with anticipation. Yet she knew such thinking could only cause trouble, and when she climbed into bed later that night, she told herself firmly that she needed to focus on locking her feelings away.

But when she fell asleep, she dreamed of him.

Cade was awake, drinking his first cup of coffee in the kitchen when the lights from Mariah's car swept over the windows. He glanced at the wall clock over the fridge.

Five o'clock.

He shook his head, his gaze tracking the glow of taillights as her car crossed the bridge, the red gleam growing fainter until it disappeared as the vehicle followed the lane around the bulge of a butte. *Crazy hour for a woman to go to work.*

He carried his coffee down the hall to the office and settled behind the desk. He booted up his laptop and went online, searching the web for rodeo schedules.

Neither he, Ned Anderson nor the investigator had located Brodie yet and Cade had a bad feeling about his brother. A competitor at Brodie's level didn't just drop off the rodeo circuit—not unless he'd been hurt.

He'd resigned himself to waiting for Zach to hike back down the mountain and return to cell phone zones although he had no idea how long that would be. And he knew Eli would surface, sooner or later. More than twelve months had already passed since Eli had last been heard from, so Cade figured he should be checking in pretty soon.

But Brodie—yeah, he thought, he was definitely starting to get worried about Brodie.

Maybe I should change the search parameters, he thought.

A half hour later, Cade had a hit. A few lines in a New Mexico newspaper told him Brodie had been injured in a riding accident. The date of injury was several months earlier. He couldn't tell from the brief sentences whether Brodie had recovered, but at least his name wasn't in the obituary column.

No wonder we couldn't find him on the circuit, he thought, a sharp twinge of concern twisting in his gut. *He hasn't been riding.*

He copied the information and pasted it into an email, then forwarded it to the attorney's and investigator's offices.

He glanced at his watch, frustrated when he calculated time zones and realized it was too early for records offices to be open at hospitals in New Mexico.

He thrust his fingers through his hair and raked it back off his forehead in frustration. Much as he wanted to find Brodie, there was too much to do at the ranch to spend his days searching, not when the attorney and investigator were on top of the situation. This was one of those times when he needed to delegate, although when it came to his brothers, he wanted to be hands-on.

He shoved back his chair and headed for the front door. Grabbing his hat and slipping into his coat, he left the house. Long strides carried him quickly across the yard toward the bunkhouse, where lights gleamed from the windows, telling him Pete was awake and hopefully, had breakfast started.

Conversation over dinner in the bunkhouse that evening focused on Joseph and Melanie Coulter's enthusiasm for collecting. Cade answered questions from the three but didn't volunteer information on his own.

Mariah was intrigued to learn that several of the locked buildings on the property had been used by Cade's parents to store collections. They'd gathered saddles, tack, Pendleton blankets, antique conveyances that ranged from buckboards to stagecoaches—and given Cade's reticence, Mariah suspected there were further collections. Joseph's will had left specific collections to each of his sons but Cade didn't elaborate on who got what.

Not for the first time since hearing Indian Springs residents tell stories about Melanie Coulter, Mariah reflected that she must have been a fascinating woman and when she was alive, Joseph must have been a far different man than the sad, quiet man she herself had known before he died.

When they rose from the table, Mariah carried her plate and utensils to the kitchen area along with the men but Pete insisted he was going to clean the kitchen.

Since she'd cooked dinner, Mariah didn't argue, saying good-night before taking her coat from the pegs just inside the door.

"I'll walk out with you," Cade said behind her.

Mariah immediately picked up on an undertone in Cade's voice.

"Fine," she replied with a forced smile. He donned his Stetson and coat while she wrapped a muffler around her neck and slipped into her jacket, tugging on her gray wool hat.

He pulled open the door and she went out, drawing on her gloves as she walked. Cade stepped out onto the porch behind her, pacing quietly behind her down the steps, then striding beside her as she set off on the lane to her house. The full moon high above them was a bright globe in the starlit sky, the clear silvery light casting dark shadows across the landscape.

Cade waited until they were several yards away from the bunkhouse before speaking.

"I'm borrowing a couple of pack mules from Jed Turner," he told her. "And he's going along to help hunt for cattle. I'm not sure how many of his brothers will be with us, but probably at least a couple. Which means," he continued, glancing sideways at her, "we'll have plenty of riders to cover the pastures and chase cows. You can stay home with a clear conscience."

She stopped abruptly, looking up at him. "I don't want to stay home."

A flicker of impatience moved over his features. "Why the hell do you want to spend a week or more combing pastures, spending long hours in the saddle and sleeping on hard ground that's likely going to be cold and wet?"

"Because I don't want special privileges for being female," she told him. "I promised Joseph I would do whatever I could to help his sons hold the ranch. He wanted you all to return to Montana—and stay on the land where Coulters had lived for over a hundred years."

"But you *are* a female," he said flatly. "In my world, that makes a difference. There's no way I'm going to treat you like a man."

"I never said I wanted to be treated like a man," Mariah snapped. "I said I don't want to be discriminated against because I'm a woman."

"What discrimination?" Cade growled. "All I'm trying to do is spare you hard work under what will probably be miserable conditions. What's wrong with that?"

"Nothing—if I had a broken arm or leg and needed care. But I'm a healthy woman, capable of riding a horse and chasing cows." She glared at him. "This isn't 1850, you know. Women have rights."

He snorted and muttered something inaudible under his breath.

Mariah couldn't quite make out his words but she had a pretty good idea what he meant.

"Why am I not surprised that you don't value a woman's right to independence?" she said with a huff of annoyance.

"You're wrong," he stated. "I value it. My mother was one of the most independent people I've ever known. But that didn't keep her from letting my dad open doors for her or doing heavy lifting." His green eyes fairly glowed with heat. "Because she was smart—and rational—and reasonable." He bent nearer. "Men respected her because she commanded respect. Not because she filed a lawsuit to compel it."

Mariah opened her mouth to protest, to tell him that she agreed with what he was saying, but he spoke before she could form the words.

"You can go cattle hunting with us, Ms. Jones. And you'll get your wish—I'll treat you just like the men. You'd better be damn sure you're as good as they are."

He turned on his heel and stalked toward the ranch house. Mariah could only watch him go, speechless.

His tall, broad figure climbed the porch to the main house and disappeared inside.

Mariah turned, trudging the rest of the way to her cabin. As she went through her normal nighttime routine, she couldn't help but wonder if she'd made a mistake with Cade. She'd ridden out with Pete and J.T. on day trips before and always enjoyed the work. If Cade was determined, however, she was sure he could make the roundup an uncomfortable experience for her.

But would he? She set her alarm and switched off the bedside lamp, staring at the moonlit white ceiling as she pondered the wisdom of insisting on going on the roundup when the boss had specifically said he didn't want her there.

Instinct told her, however, that though he seemed convinced she'd be better off staying at home, Cade Coulter wouldn't purposely go out of his way to make her miserable. Just how she knew that, she wasn't sure, but there was something intrinsically honorable about him.

Reassured, she curled on her side and closed her eyes.

Chapter Six

Cade met with Ned Anderson the following afternoon.

"Have you found out where Brodie went when he left
New Mexico?" he asked after declining a drink.

"Not yet. I talked to the investigator just before you
got here and he says it's as if Brodie walked out of the
hospital and disappeared into thin air."

"Damn." Cade removed his hat and dropped it on
the floor beside his chair, raking one hand through his
hair. "Where the hell is he?" His gaze sharpened over
the attorney. "What did the hospital records say about
his injuries?"

"Broken arm and a few cracked ribs," Ned said. "The
doctor who signed his release said Brodie left over his
medical objections but he was walking. Nothing life
threatening, evidently."

Ned rocked back in his chair, crossing his hands over his round belly, and eyed Cade over the rims of his glasses. "I hope the investigator finds some leads soon. Due to the manner in which your father split the assets of the ranch among you four, all of your brothers need to be found as soon as possible."

"I know." Cade rested one booted foot on the opposite knee, frowning. "It's possible we could raise enough money to pay off the taxes if we auctioned off Mom and Dad's collections. But that's not doable without everyone's permission."

"Have you been inside the storage barns and the Lodge or cabins?" Ned asked.

"No. I checked the buildings to make sure they were structurally sound with solid walls and roofs but decided to leave it to my brothers to investigate the contents."

"I suspect there may be auctionable items in your mother's studio." Ned considered Cade, his eyes shrewd. "Her work was worth a great deal before she died and has only increased in value since the accident. I believe Joseph told me that he sealed her studio on the ranch the day of her funeral and no one has been inside since, is that correct?"

Cade nodded silently.

"I cannot give the studio key to anyone but Eli, officially," Ned continued. "But if the structure were unsound in some way and you needed to make repairs, as executor of the estate, I would certainly understand the necessity of you entering the building."

The attorney's inference was clear. But Cade shook his head.

"Much as I'd like to know whether Mom left something that might save the ranch, Ned, I can't do it. At least not yet," he added. "If Eli doesn't check in before long, I'll consider it."

The attorney shrugged. "Your choice, Cade. I wouldn't have suggested you verify contents if I didn't know how badly your father wanted to see his sons back on the Triple C. Losing the ranch to taxes never occurred to him, at least as far as I know. He was concerned with leaving each of you something of your mother's in addition to equal shares in the land itself. That was his main focus."

"Too bad he wasn't as concerned about us when we were kids."

"It's my personal belief that he regretted his actions when you boys were young," Ned told him, his voice carefully neutral. "Unfortunately, he didn't come to that realization until you were all grown and gone."

"Maybe." Cade's skepticism rang in his deep voice. "Or maybe he didn't have anyone else to leave the place to."

"Perhaps." The attorney sat forward and pulled a file toward him. "I wanted to let you know that the investigative agency has a potential lead on Eli's whereabouts."

Cade's gaze sharpened and he leaned forward slightly. "What is it?"

"They've located a young woman who apprenticed with him under a silversmith in an artist's colony in New Mexico. Interestingly enough, Eli was living not far from where Brodie was hospitalized, and during the same time frame."

"Maybe Brodie was down there visiting Eli," Cade said. "He did that when he was traveling—if he had a rodeo near where one of us was living, he'd call and we'd get together."

"Well, we don't know for sure if that's why Brodie was in the area," Ned told him. "And the young woman doesn't know Brodie but she remembers Eli very well." Ned smiled. "She apparently had a bit of a crush on him."

"That doesn't surprise me," Cade said drily. "Women always love Eli."

"In any event, she thought he left the colony to travel overseas for an apprenticeship."

"Did she know where specifically?"

Ned shook his head. "No, but the agency is sending an investigator to check out the organization in New Mexico. Hopefully, we'll learn more soon." He flipped the file closed. "Has your brother Zach contacted you yet?"

"No." Cade stood. "But at least I know where he is and that it's only a matter of time before he calls."

"Yes, thank goodness. I'll let you know immediately if we receive any further information about Brodie or Eli." Ned stood, too, and the men shook hands.

As Cade left the office, he wondered grimly how much longer it might take to find his brothers and if the Triple C could hold on until they surfaced.

He drove down Main Street but when he reached the edge of town, instead of accelerating toward the Triple C, he slowed. He turned left, driving between two white pillars and past a sign telling visitors they'd just entered the Indian Springs Cemetery.

He'd driven down the narrow gravel lane between green lawns dotted with headstones dozens of times when he was a teenager. He and his brothers had made this their last stop before they left town thirteen years earlier.

Cade wasn't sure why he'd put off coming here since he'd returned but when he left the truck and walked across the dried winter grass to his mother's grave, the realization hit him hard.

There were two gravestones now.

The white marble marker at the head of Joseph's grave was simple, with only his name and the dates marking the year he was born, and the year he died. The shape and size matched Melanie's exactly.

He knew he was supposed to feel something—grief, anger…something. But he felt nothing.

Car tires crunched on the gravel of the drive behind him but he didn't turn around.

A door closed with a quiet *thunk,* footsteps making small noises as a person walked across the grass.

Cade wasn't in the mood to chat and make polite conversation. He hoped whoever was behind him moved on without talking.

"Cade…"

Mariah's soft voice snapped his head around. She stood a few feet away, her arms cradling two large bundles of flowers. A black wool coat covered her from her throat to below her knees, her feet covered in warm winter boots and black wool gloves on her hands. The breeze skeined strands of her loose hair over her cheek and she lifted a hand, brushing them back. The blond strands gleamed like bright silver against the black wool of her coat.

"I'm sorry to intrude," she apologized, her brown eyes warm with empathy. She gestured with the bundle of flowers at the headstones. "I stopped to leave some flowers—do you mind?"

"Not at all," he said. "Go ahead."

She bent to remove wilted flowers from the metal holder mounted at the side of the headstones. She laid them aside and as she tucked new stems with fresh flowers into the holders, Cade realized that he hadn't registered the flowers earlier.

And they were daisies.

His mother's favorite flower.

"How did you know to bring her daisies?" he asked, bemused.

"Joseph told me that she loved daisies. He came here every Sunday afternoon, all year-round, and brought her flowers—he always gave her daisies." Mariah looked up at him, a soft, sad smile curving her lush mouth. "He never missed a week. At the end, he fretted and worried when he was too ill to leave his bed so I brought the flowers. I told him I'd visit and bring daisies when he was gone." She glanced at the two matching headstones before looking back at Cade. "He loved her very much," she said softly.

"He loved her too damned much." Cade knew his voice was too detached, with too little feeling in contrast to her emotion, but he couldn't pretend something he didn't feel. And what he felt was—nothing. There was a cold void where his heart should be.

Mariah's eyes widened in surprise. "How can a husband love a wife too much?"

"When he tries to climb into the grave with her. When he wishes he'd died with her," Cade said in that oddly unemotional voice. "When he goes crazy with grief at her loss and tries to destroy himself and everyone who ever loved her."

"Is that what Joseph did when your mother died?" Mariah sounded shaken.

"Pretty much." Cade realized he'd shocked her. He should have let her keep her illusions about his father. "It's not something you should worry about," he told her, shrugging. He nodded at the flowers that filled the vases. "Are you finished here?"

"Yes, I, um…" She glanced at the wilted, dry stems in her hands as if she'd forgotten she held them. "I guess I am."

"I'll walk you back to your car."

She didn't object when he stepped back to let her walk past him, then fell into step beside her. When they reached her vehicle, parked in front of his truck, he pulled open the door and waited as she settled in the driver's seat.

"Drive carefully," he told her. He bent to tuck the bottom hem of her coat inside and gently closed the door.

He felt her gaze on him and knew she watched him in her rearview mirror as he walked to his truck and got in. By the time he twisted the key and the engine turned over, she was moving, pulling out of the cemetery and onto the highway toward the Triple C.

She probably thinks I'm a cold son of a bitch, he thought as he followed.

He was sorry for that. But he'd locked away all emotions over his father years ago. Even if he wanted to, he didn't think he could pull them out now.

Some things were better left buried.

That evening, Mariah was wiping down the stove and J.T. had just finished drying and putting away the last dish in the kitchen when a truck drove up outside.

"We have visitors," Pete commented. He set down

the deck of cards and the box of poker chips on the table before crossing the room to pull open the door. "Hey, what are you three doing out this late?"

"Evenin', Pete." Boots thudded on the porch boards and Pete stepped back, holding the door wide as Asa, Ben and Wayne entered.

"Hi, Cade, Mariah, J.T." Ben grinned, winking at Mariah. "Thought we'd take you up on your invitation and drop by," he told Cade.

"Glad to see you, Ben." Cade gestured at the table. "You're just in time—we're about to play poker." He crossed the room to collect more chairs and carried them back to the table. "Did you bring money?"

"Ha," Wayne snorted. "Seems to me I remember you asking me that before, from the time you were about twelve and you started winning all my money and emptying my pockets."

"But up until then, you kept taking my nickels," Cade reminded him. "You said it was an important part of the lesson and since you were teaching me to play poker, you were required to teach me about losing."

"That's right." Wayne's eyes twinkled. "But you soon started winning back those nickels."

"I had to," Cade told him. "I was losing my school lunch money."

"Geez, Wayne," Asa said. "You took the kid's lunch money?"

"I didn't keep it," Wayne protested. "I dropped the nickels in a jar and Cade won every one of them back."

"In the meantime, I had to eat peanut butter sandwiches for about six months."

"Doesn't look like it had any long-term bad effects,"

Wayne told him, clapping him on the shoulder. "You're not too puny."

Cade laughed. "No, I guess not. How about something to drink before we get started?" he asked, leading the way into the kitchen.

"Evening, Mariah," Asa said as the kitchen area filled with men.

"Hi, Asa." Mariah smiled at him with genuine affection. She had a soft spot in her heart for Joseph's three old friends. "There's fresh coffee, if you want some, or there's beer and soda in the fridge."

"I think I'll have a longneck," he told her. "Ben's the designated driver tonight, though, so he'll probably have coffee."

"Yep, I'd better." Ben slung an arm over her shoulder and gave her a quick, friendly hug. "How you been, darlin'?"

"Good, Ben," she responded. "I'm good."

"I hope you brought your piggy bank," he told her with a wink. "'Cause I'm feelin' lucky tonight."

"I'm not sure I want to play cards with you three. I've heard you telling stories in the café and it sounded to me like you're all card sharks."

Ben pressed his hand over his heart. "Me? No, no, no, not when we play with friends."

"Hmm." Mariah eyed him skeptically as she took a soda from the fridge and handed him a longneck bottle of beer. "I'll believe that when I see it."

"You'd better sit next to me, Mariah," Pete told her, blue eyes filled with amusement. "Ben has been known to cheat."

"That's a downright lie," his friend said promptly and without heat. "Now if you're talking about Wayne or Asa—there's no question it pays to keep your eye on them."

Mariah took her seat as the three older men settled into chairs and wrangled amiably over who was most likely to play poker by the book. She glanced across the table and met Cade's amused gaze, their shared enjoyment of the men's friendly argument creating a bond that felt so right. The strength of the bond surprised her and she looked away, unsure what had just happened between them.

"Ante up." Cade's voice pulled her attention away from her thoughts.

"What are we playing?" J.T. asked.

"Stud poker."

I should have known, Mariah thought as she tossed a penny into the center of the table with the rest of the players. *How appropriate.*

An hour later, money had changed hands and fickle Lady Luck had smiled without prejudice on first one, then another of the players. No one had enjoyed a steady streak of good luck, though, and the piles of chips and pennies in front of the players were roughly the same as when they'd started.

"I need a break," Mariah announced. "Anyone want cake and ice cream?"

A chorus of cheers made her smile. J.T. followed her into the kitchen to carry filled plates back to the table. When everyone had dessert in front of them, Mariah slipped again into her chair and picked up her fork.

"Asa, do you know if Dad sold the Kigers?" Cade asked.

His question grabbed her attention and she exchanged a quick interested look with J.T. before focusing on Asa.

"I never heard that he did," Asa replied. "On the other hand, I never heard that he didn't, either." He looked at Ben and Wayne. "Did you two ever hear anyone say they bought the Kigers?"

The two men shook their heads.

"I think we would have heard about it," Ben said. "Those Kigers of your mom's were valuable horses."

"What are Kigers, exactly?" J.T. asked. "I've heard of quarterhorses, thoroughbreds, Morgans and a long list of other breeds but I've never known anyone who mentioned Kigers."

"They're Mustangs," Cade told him.

"They're pretty much the Cadillac of Mustangs," Wayne added. "They were named after the Kiger Gorge at Steens Mountain range in Oregon where they live. There are lots of Mustang herds across the West—especially in Utah and Nevada—but the Mustangs isolated in the Steens Mountains are special."

"Beautiful horses," Asa put in, shaking his head as his eyes fogged with memories. "I remember a pinto your mama used to ride, Cade. Sweetest little filly I ever saw."

"Mom loved those horses," Cade agreed with a small reminiscent smile. "She and Dad used to argue about whether her Mustangs were as good as his quarterhorses."

"She kept the pinto at home to ride but pastured the rest of the herd up on Tunk Mountain," Ben said, eyes narrowed as he remembered. "We rode up there with her and Joseph a couple of times, me and Wayne."

"Where did she get them?" Mariah asked, fascinated by this window into Cade's parents and his past.

"Bought them from the government," Wayne told her.

"The government?" She must have looked as confused as she felt because Wayne grinned at her.

"Wild Mustangs are protected by the federal government—they run free on government land. Every year or so, when the herds get too big, the government rounds up some of them and auctions them off."

"They only auction the Kigers every few years," Asa put in. "The herds are smaller so there aren't as many colts to sell but every time there's a Kiger auction, folks turn out in droves. Over the years, Melanie gathered a small herd of her own with a stallion and mares, several colts. She wanted them to thrive and live much as they were accustomed to in Oregon, so she pastured them in the wildest part of the Triple C. Tunk Mountain is part of that farthest pasture."

"What happened to your mom's little pinto filly, Cade?" Ben asked.

"Dad rode out with her on a lead rope the day after Mom's funeral. He was gone overnight. He came back without her."

A small silence fell following Cade's short reply.

"I always thought he took her out and shot her," Cade continued, the blunt words falling into the silence. "But maybe he took her up on Tunk Mountain and turned her loose with the rest of the Kigers."

"You think they might still be up there?" J.T. asked, his eyes gleaming with interest. "Running wild?"

"Hard to say." Cade shrugged. "One thing's for sure—if they were, no one would ever know. If Dad never rounded up the stray cattle beyond the home pastures, it's not likely he would have kept track of the Kigers. Tunk Mountain's too far out."

"We should ride up there," Ben put in. "Check it out."

"Yeah," Asa and Wayne chimed in.

"Even if we had time, which we don't," Cade said, "I'd still have to wait for Brodie."

"How come?" Wayne asked.

"Because Dad's will left the horses to Brodie. He's the one that should go looking for the Kigers."

"I thought Joseph left you all the stock?" Pete said, his gaze questioning.

"He left me everything except the horses," Cade corrected him. "I didn't think there were any horses except Sarge. But," he added, "if the Kigers are still there, maybe there are a lot of horses."

"I'd sure like to find out." Ben's eyes sparkled with interest. "How long before Brodie gets home?"

"I wish I knew." A faint frown darkened Cade's green eyes. "We haven't found him yet."

"Damn." Ben's eyes dimmed.

"Well," Asa said bracingly when another silence stretched as they all contemplated the worrisome lack of information about Cade's brother. "Nothing we can do about it now—so let's get on with the poker game. I need to win some coffee money for tomorrow morning."

Chapter Seven

Three days later, the Triple C crew and four of the Turner brothers left the ranch just after 6:00 a.m. Mariah rode with Pete in his old but sturdy truck as they left the graded ranch road and set off across the pasture. They were the second vehicle in the caravan with Cade leading the way and two Turner ranch trucks bringing up the rear. Each of the trucks pulled horse trailers and the pickup beds were loaded with camping equipment and tack.

She glanced in the side mirror. The trucks behind were bumping and rocking along the track, their speed steady as they followed Cade's lead.

"How long did Cade say we'd have to drive before we leave the trucks and unload the horses?" she asked Pete, settling forward in her seat once again.

"At least an hour, probably more. The only way in is

to go through the pastures and the road isn't a straight shot, winds all over the place—otherwise we'd be there a lot sooner."

It seemed to Mariah that it took forever before they crossed the home pasture, passed through a wire gate and drove deeper into the second one. Almost immediately, it became obvious that no one had used this section of land for some time.

"I think I can see why Joseph kept the cattle in the pasture next to the home buildings," Mariah murmured as the land outside her window became increasingly rough. The track they drove on now was barely more than a cow path and before long, the taillights on Cade's pickup ahead of them flashed as he braked, then turned right onto an open, flat space.

Pete followed him, the truck bumping and lurching over the uneven ground. He pulled up beside Cade's truck just as he and J.T. were leaving the cab and Pete rolled down his window.

"Is this Coyote Creek?"

"No," Cade replied, settling his Stetson lower on his brow. "But the terrain gets a lot rougher about a quarter mile from here and given how bad the road is up to here, I don't want to chance taking the trucks farther. We'll ride the rest of the way."

Pete nodded and switched off his engine. He glanced sideways at Mariah and a boyish grin lit his face. "Well, girl, it's time to cowboy-up."

She laughed, rolled her eyes at him, and shoved open her door. "I'm ready, ace."

His deep chuckle reached her ears as her boots hit the ground and she headed for the back of the horse trailer.

Mariah stayed out of the men's way as they unloaded mules and horses from the trailers and strapped loaded pack boxes on the mules. She backed her own mare out of the trailer behind Pete's truck and walked her several yards away from the busy area in front of the trucks. She'd loaded Zelda into Pete's trailer saddled and haltered for transport; now she stripped off the mare's halter and slid the bit between her teeth, buckling the straps. Zelda stamped and nudged her muzzle against Mariah's shoulder, whickering softly.

"Patience, Zelda," Mariah whispered. "We'll be moving soon."

The air was chilly and she tucked her chin into her muffler for warmth, leaning into Zelda's warm side. The mare *whuffed* in acknowledgment but didn't look at Mariah, her intelligent brown gaze fixed on the activity as Cade, Pete, J.T. and the four Turner brothers tightened cinches and checked the load distribution on the backs of the two mules.

"We're ready, boss," Pete called.

Cade ran an assessing glance over the mules, horses and riders. Mariah felt the heat of his gaze for a brief moment before he looked away.

"Well, Zelda," she muttered so only the mare could hear. "That's one way for a woman to warm up." The horse's ears swiveled in response but she stood rock still as Mariah put her foot in the stirrup, grabbed the saddle horn and swung into the saddle.

"Everybody else ready to leave?" Cade asked, one swift glance confirming nods of agreement before he stepped into the saddle. Jiggs danced beneath him, eager to be gone, but Cade controlled him with a quiet word and a firm hand on the reins.

Mariah's mare was well mannered and stood calmly while the others swung aboard. Cade led the way, followed by J.T. and the four Turners with the pack mules, while Mariah and Pete brought up the rear.

The crisp early morning air was invigorating. Bundled as she was in coat, hat, gloves and muffler, Mariah was comfortable and able to enjoy the ride. Still, she was ready to step down when they reached Coyote Creek and dismounted to set up camp. The small grove of trees lining the creek widened here and a holding pen made of weathered poles crossed the banks to enclose a section of water. New wood stood out in several places against the gray older poles, silent testimony to the hours Cade and J.T. had spent making the fence sturdy over the last few days.

Within an hour, the crew had unloaded the pack boxes, set up camp, hobbled the mules and were ready to hunt cows.

"We'll split up in teams of two and work the west quarter of the pasture nearest camp," Cade said, handing each of them a sheet of paper with the pasture fence lines clearly drawn and the acres divided into fourths. "Drive any cattle you find back here and into the holding corrals. Anybody want to volunteer to break early and come back to start supper?"

"I will, boss," Pete responded.

"Thanks, Pete. Anybody have any questions?" Cade's gaze met each of the others and got a shake of the head each time. "Then let's split up."

"I'll go with Pete," Mariah chimed in. During the drive from the house, Pete had agreed to partner with her.

Cade looked at the old cowboy and Pete nodded his head in agreement.

"All right. J.T., you'll come with me." He looked at Jed and grinned. "Which of your little brothers are you taking with you?"

There was an instant chorus of derisive comments from Ash, Dallas and Grady Turner and Jed grinned.

"I'll take Grady," he drawled. "He's least likely to fall off his horse."

There were more pithy comments and Mariah hid a smile at the creative swear words. The Turners were still heckling their oldest brother when they left the group, two by two, to search their assigned section of land.

She reined Zelda after Pete into a sagebrush-dotted stretch of prairie, bisected by the indent of a winding coulee.

Pete paused, standing in his stirrups to sweep the open land with a searching look. "Hard to tell what's out there. What do you say we follow the coulee for a while?"

"Seems like a good place for cows to hide," Mariah agreed.

They ate lunch sitting in their saddles, keeping an eye on the six cow-calf pairs and three steers they'd located. By the time they herded the day's collection back to the corral, the number of cattle had grown to twelve mama cows with twelve calves at their sides and six steers.

"I'm surprised at the number of cattle we found," Pete said as he swung the corral gate closed. "I sure didn't expect this many."

"Me, either," Mariah said, hope surging. "If everyone else has this much luck, Cade should be able to generate a solid profit for the Triple C."

"Yep." Pete nodded, his blue eyes gleaming with satisfaction. He lifted his battered cowboy hat, rubbed a hand over his thinning hair, and resettled the brim back over his brow. "We'd better get dinner started. The crew's bound to be hungry by the time they get back."

"Let's make a pot of coffee for us first," Mariah said, falling in step with him as he walked toward the camp. "There ought to be some benefits to pulling kitchen patrol tonight."

Pete glanced down at her and grinned. "Girl, I like the way you think."

The sun was hovering on the horizon when Cade and J.T., the last of the crew to arrive, drove more than a dozen head of cattle toward the corral.

Mariah and Pete, Jed, Grady, Ash and Dallas were gathered around the campfire, tin mugs of coffee in their hands. The noise of cattle had them getting up to head to the corral. Dallas pulled open the gate as the small herd neared and Cade and J.T. drove them inside.

The two riders swung off their horses, lifting stirrups to hook them over the saddlehorns so they could unbuckle girths.

"How many did you find, Cade?" Jed asked.

"Twenty-two." Cade glanced over his shoulder, his green gaze sweeping the men until he found Mariah. He raked her from head to toe with a quick glance. Then he turned back to Jiggs, pulling saddle and pad off the big black to carry them to the cleared space around the fire. "How about the rest of you?"

It turned out Mariah and Pete had found the most with their thirty. Nevertheless, the total of all the cattle was far higher than anyone had expected.

Cade's green eyes gleamed with satisfaction. "If every

section has this many cattle, this drive is going to be well worth the effort."

"Damned straight," Pete commented. "And it's a good thing because I'd hate to be doin' this much work and sleepin' on hard ground for nothin'." His matter-of-fact tone didn't entirely conceal his delight that he and Mariah had brought in the highest number of cows. He jerked his thumb over his shoulder, indicating the portable camp stove and the tripod with an iron Dutch oven suspended over the fire. "Supper's ready. Better come and get it while it's hot."

The rest of the crew had eaten earlier but they filled mugs with hot coffee and sat around the fire while Cade and J.T. ate plates of stew and baking powder biscuits.

"I wasn't sure it was possible Joseph would really have ignored strays and let cattle run wild. But after the number of cows we saw today, I'm starting to believe that's exactly what he did." Dallas Turner sat cross-legged on the saddle blanket he'd spread on the ground, cradling a hot mug in his hands. "What I don't understand is—why?"

"Maybe he didn't need the money," Ash said, venturing a guess at a possible answer to his brother's question.

"No." Pete shook his head. "That's not it. Joseph was dead broke when he died."

"If he needed the money, it makes even less sense." Dallas turned his gaze on Cade. "Do you know why your dad didn't round up cattle out here, Cade?"

Cade shook his head. "I've been gone for thirteen years. I have no idea why Dad did what he did, or didn't do, during that time."

"You never talked to him?" Grady's keen gaze studied Cade.

Mariah expected Cade would show some reaction to being questioned about Joseph, but she could discern no emotion at all on his features.

"No."

"Huh." Grady stared into the fire, apparently baffled by both Joseph and Cade. "What about your brothers? Did any of them talk with him?"

"Not that I know of."

And he would know if they had, Mariah thought with sudden conviction. Although Cade had told her the brothers got in touch only once a year or so, she had the impression that they remained close.

The conversation moved on to other subjects, the night falling full dark around them. Much as she enjoyed listening to the others, Mariah soon found herself stifling yawns. She'd been awake before dawn, spent a long day riding in crisp fresh air, and with her stomach full of hearty food, weariness was catching up with her.

"I think I'll turn in," she said during a lull in the conversation. "It's been a long day."

"Good night, Mariah." Grady Turner's deep drawl was polite, a friendly smile lighting his handsome face. "I sure hope you're making the coffee again in the morning, 'cause if Dallas does it, none of us will be able to drink it."

"Aw, hell," Dallas said with disgust. "Don't listen to him, Mariah, my coffee's just fine."

"Neither one of you can make decent coffee," Jed put in. "If Renee hadn't banned you two from the kitchen, we'd have shot you both years ago."

Mariah laughed and walked away from the camp-fire, leaving the Turners good-naturedly wrangling. Cade watched them with an amused half smile, J.T. seemed baffled by their friendly harassment and Pete chuckled.

Several yards away from the crew, Mariah crawled into her sleeping bag, spread out next to Pete's. Cade had dropped her saddle there earlier and she rolled up her jacket, tucking it against the leather saddle seat for a pillow. She lay with her feet stretched toward the fire and at the moment, was toasty warm. Nevertheless, she suspected that after midnight, just before dawn, she'd likely have the down bag pulled over her chin to stay warm.

She stared up at the black bowl of night sky. A quarter moon had risen and rode just above the horizon while myriad stars glittered and sparkled across the dark arch of sky, so clear and bright that Mariah would swear she could touch them.

But she was too tired to stretch out her arms and try. Her eyelashes weighted her lids and they drifted lower. At last, they became too heavy to hold up and her eyes closed. She drifted to sleep with the deep murmur of men's voices and Cade's occasional laughter the last thing she heard.

Chapter Eight

Much to her delight, Mariah woke the next morning to find a warm wind blowing. A Montana chinook had brought warmer temperatures overnight and the remaining snow was melting quickly beneath sunshine and wind. By noon, she'd shed her coat and tied it behind the saddle.

The day was spent much like the prior one and Pete beamed at the number of cows they collected in their section of pasture. Late that evening, Mariah left the rest of the crew around the campfire, swapping stories about roping steers. Each tale grew more outrageous and bursts of laughter reached her as she brushed Zelda. Dusk had fallen and she'd pulled on a hooded red sweater to ward off the chill of evening.

"Tired of hearing roping stories?" Cade's deep voice came out of the darkness.

She glanced over her shoulder to see him walking toward her from the far end of the horse enclosure. He carried the enamel coffeepot, droplets of water falling from the blue surface as he walked.

"No, I wanted to brush Zelda before I went to bed." She pointed at the wet enamelware. "Are you taking over kitchen duty?"

His chuckle sent a shiver of awareness over her sensitized skin.

"No, not hardly. I volunteered to rinse out the pot upstream." He set the container atop a fence post and shoved his hand into his jacket pocket, pulling out a carrot. "Hey, Zelda," he murmured. He snapped the carrot into pieces and laid a chunk on the flat of his palm before holding out his hand to her. "Want a treat?"

The mare immediately reached out and lipped the chunk from his palm.

The clip-clop of shod hooves sounded and Mariah looked past Zelda's hindquarters. Jiggs walked toward them, ears swiveling, his dark intelligent eyes fixed on Cade.

"Hey, boy." Cade fed him a chunk of carrot and rubbed the stallion's head beneath his forelock.

"He's very smart, isn't he?" Mariah spoke softly, continuing to stroke the brush over Zelda's tangled mane.

"I think so." Cade fed the two horses the rest of the carrot. "That's it, Jiggs, no more." He took a brush from the bucket outside the fence and joined Mariah, sweeping long strokes over Zelda's hide. Zelda swung her head to look at him, bumped her muzzle against his shoulder, and faced front again, her eyes half closed with pleasure.

Cade grinned at Mariah. "She likes being brushed?"

"Oh, yes. She loves it."

The two worked in companionable silence, one on each side of the mare, until Mariah ducked under Zelda's neck and unintentionally came up within the spread of Cade's arms.

She froze, the mare at her back and Cade only inches away in front of her.

Mariah lifted her gaze, feeling her eyes widen as she saw his green eyes reflect surprise before they darkened, heat swirling in the emerald depths.

Zelda shifted, bumping Mariah forward and against Cade.

"I'm sorry," Mariah whispered, trying to move back but unable to because of the bulk of the mare.

"I'm not." His voice rasped, rougher, deeper.

The sound of it shivered over her skin, rippling against nerves already strung taut.

His head lowered, his mouth nearly touching hers.

She was dizzy with the scent of leather and faint aftershave, clean soap and the slight tang of coffee on his warm breath where it brushed her lips.

"Hey, Cade! You out there?"

Mariah jerked backward, bumping Zelda, who reacted by nickering with surprise and sidestepping.

Cade caught Mariah's waist and pulled her away from the mare, shifting her sideways and behind him.

"Yeah—what do you need, Pete?"

"Just wanted to see if you're done rinsing my coffeepot—I want to fill it before I head for bed," the old cowboy called back.

"Be right there." Cade turned, looking down at Mariah.

"I'd better go," Mariah said quickly. She slipped under the fencing and picked up the bucket. "Good night," she said over her shoulder, her gaze meeting his for a fleeting moment before she walked away.

She returned the bucket of brushes and hoof picks to its place by the pack boxes and called good-night to the men around the fire before crawling into her sleeping bag.

She was sure he'd been about to kiss her. Lots of men had wanted to kiss her. But she'd wanted Cade's kiss. Badly.

She wasn't sure how she felt about that. Nor how she'd feel if he never tried again.

The warmer weather held over the following days as the crew combed the far-flung acres in search of more cattle. The herd held in the corral grew larger by the day. Each morning, the crew left the camp in twos, pairing up to ride the breaks, hills, prairie and coulees.

Just before noon one day, Cade and Jed climbed a low hill and scanned the land below.

"I'll be damned. I don't believe what I'm seeing." Cade thumbed the brim of his Stetson back and stared at the small herd of cattle in the draw below them.

"Those are longhorns—and Brahmas. I didn't know Joseph had any—everything we've found so far are Herefords," Jed said, studying the big bull and his harem of cows. The massive male was clearly a mixed breed with a Brahma hump, longhorn ears and mostly brown coat mottled with white. All of the females had young calves at their sides.

"Look at the horns on that bull." Cade pointed at

a huge bull. "They must be five feet from tip-to-tip, easy."

"At least," Jed agreed. "Damn. He's somethin', isn't he?" He grinned and looked at Cade. "I'd hate like hell to get near those horns. That bull could skewer a man like a barbecue spit."

"And he could gut a horse from chest to tail with one twist of his head." Cade muttered an oath. "I have no idea how many like him are out here but I don't want anybody getting hurt so nobody goes near the longhorns, especially not Mariah or J.T."

"Makes sense," Jed conceded. "They won't complain if you ban all the crew from chasing the longhorns but if you single those two out, you'll catch flak."

"Then none of us will round them up." Cade didn't want Mariah anywhere near the potentially dangerous cattle. "We'll get as many of the Herefords as we can find and after we've trailed them home, plan another trip to get the longhorns. And we won't bring Mariah with us."

"Sounds good," Jed said.

"Let's head back. We'll pick up the others and comb the draws to the east of here. Tonight I'll tell them about the longhorns."

Cade waited until dinner was over and the eight wranglers were sitting around the campfire, cradling cups of hot coffee, before broaching the subject of the longhorns.

"You're kidding." J.T.'s expression matched the astonishment in his voice. "I've never seen longhorns on the Triple C. I don't remember Joseph ever mentioning he had any, either. Where did they come from?"

"Dad bought a small herd when I was a little

kid—maybe twenty-five years ago," Cade said. "He'd planned to experiment with crossbreeding longhorns with Brahmas for rodeo stock. He didn't want them crossing with the Herefords so he kept the whitefaces in the pastures nearest the house and barns. Dad turned the longhorns and Brahma cows loose out here, which put two strong fences and acres of pasture between the two."

"Do you think the longhorns you saw today are what's left of that herd?" Pete asked.

Cade shrugged. "I don't know. I remember Dad selling off a bunch of them. I was a teenager when we rounded them up that last time but I don't remember beating the bushes to make sure we got them all. I'm guessing we missed some of the bulls and cows in the first sweep and since we never went back to look again, they've been here ever since." He nodded in the direction of the Triple C's home pastures. "They're clearly a Brahma-longhorn mix but it looked to me like they've also probably bred with Herefords from the main herd, probably strays that found their way up here from the home pasture."

"How many of them do you think there are?" Mariah asked, fascinated by the idea of a herd of cattle living wild and hidden away from human eyes on the vast, untended acres of the Triple C's outer range.

"Hard to say." Cade shrugged. "Dad bought a few hundred in the original herd and I don't remember how many we rounded up and sold. I do remember that he said there should have been a higher number that year when we shipped them to the sale barn."

"So there may have been quite a few left from the original herd. Plus the calves that survived over the years since," Jed commented. "How many years since your dad sold them?"

"I think I was fifteen that year," Cade said. "So—around twenty years."

Pete whistled, a long low sound. "That's long enough for mama longhorns to have dropped a lot of babies."

"That's what I'm guessing," Cade confirmed. He glanced around the circle, meeting each pair of eyes with a hard gaze. "And they're dangerous as hell—especially the bulls. Those horns can gut a horse and rider in seconds. Which is why we're all leaving them alone. If you see one, back away and ride off."

"You don't want them driven home with the rest of the cattle we've found?" Ash Turner lifted his eyebrows, clearly surprised.

"Not now." Cade sipped his coffee, hands curled around the hot cup for warmth. "This is a fast trip to round up as many strays as we can find, drive them home, brand them, cut the bulls and sell the steers. The Triple C needs operating money, as much as I can find, as fast as I can get it. I can't afford to chance anyone getting hurt—so we'll leave the longhorns alone, for now."

Silence reigned for a moment. The fire flickered, wood snapping and cracking as it burned. Beyond the circle of light, the dark night was filled with shadows and from atop a distant butte, a coyote howled, the sound echoing over prairie, coulees and broken badlands.

"For now?" Grady Turner repeated, his eyes narrowed over Cade. "You got something planned for those longhorns in the future?"

Cade cocked his head. "Hard to say."

Grady grunted with amusement. "They're cattle,

which makes them an asset. You're a cattleman—so I'm guessing you have a plan."

"Like I said," Cade said mildly. "Hard to say."

Mariah's gaze flicked from one man to the other, fascinated by the easy interaction between Cade and the Turner brothers. Renee had said the two families of boys had grown up together and clearly, it hadn't taken them long to fall back into a casual, comfortable relationship with Cade's return.

As she listened to the men discuss the possible market for the unexpected longhorn-Brahma mixed herd and the Herefords in the corral, she wondered just how dangerous the wild cattle were. And despite the danger, she couldn't help but wish she could see one of them for herself.

As on the previous evenings in camp, Mariah was the first to climb into her sleeping bag that night. Within seconds of lying down, she was asleep, worn out by the day's riding.

When the rest of the crew said good-night and sought their own beds some time later, Cade and Pete were the only ones awake. Pete rose from his seat by the fire and hobbled to the camp stove. He was in charge of cooking and did prep work before he went to sleep each night.

Cade walked the perimeter of the corral, as he always did each evening before sleeping, checking the sturdiness of the structure. He also made a last visit to the horses and mules. He'd done the same thing with the unit of Marines he'd commanded. He never slept until he'd assured all was safe and secure.

He spent a few moments with Jiggs, brushing an empty feed sack over the stallion's back. The night was dark and Jiggs's black silhouette nearly blended into the shadows.

"Yo, boss." Pete loomed out of the shadows, carrying a sack.

"I thought you went to bed," Cade told him.

"On my way," the older cowboy replied. "I wanted to give these apple slices to the horses and mules first. Meant to give 'em apples this morning but I got busy and forgot. Didn't think of it again until just now when I took the coffee out for tomorrow and saw the bag still there."

"They'll appreciate it." Cade stretched out a hand. "I'll help, if you'd like."

"Sure." Pete held out the bag.

Jiggs lipped slices from Cade's palm. "Did you pack these apples especially for the horses?" he asked.

"No, I brought them for Mariah," Pete responded. "She loves apples but these were frostbit that first night and they're mushy. The horses and mules don't care and Mariah wouldn't complain, but she wouldn't like them as well."

"She doesn't seem to complain about anything," Cade commented.

"No, she doesn't." Pete fed slices to Sarge. "She's got grit."

"I didn't think she'd last out here." Cade glanced at the ring of sleeping bags around the fire where Mariah's bright hair gleamed against a dark saddle seat. "In fact, I'd have bet money she'd have gone home that first morning after she had to sleep on the ground. It was pretty damned cold that night."

"I knew she'd stick it out—even if it froze," Pete said with quiet assurance. "She could have left J.T. and me to fend for ourselves when Joseph was gone but she didn't. She not only stayed, she pulled her weight and worked hard." His faded blue gaze met Cade's. "J.T. and me think a lot of her. Like I said, she's got grit."

Cade nodded, acknowledging the blunt declaration of support. "I appreciate you looking out for her on this trip. When I asked you to keep an eye on her, I didn't know how good a team you'd make," Cade went on, a half smile curling his mouth. "The two of you are holding your own."

"Damned straight." Pete grinned with pride. He crumpled the empty bag. "If I'm going to hold up my end with Mariah tomorrow, I'd better head for bed. Night, boss."

"Night, Pete."

The old cowboy limped away to pull off his boots and crawl into his sleeping bag.

Cade rubbed Jiggs's neck beneath his mane and the black rested his muzzle on Cade's shoulder in companionable quiet.

Pete was right, he thought. Mariah had surprised him with her willingness to spend long hours in the saddle. She hadn't complained about the rough conditions camping out. She hadn't complained about doing her share of chores or tried to hand off her share to the men, although each of them had offered to take her jobs. She'd refused to take advantage of being the sole female in a group of men and Cade hadn't failed to notice that while all the Turners teased her, they treated her with respect and courtesy. And for hell-raisers like the Turners, that spoke volumes about their interactions with her in the past.

Jed had told him that they ate breakfast nearly every

morning at the café where Mariah worked, which meant they'd had plenty of opportunity to make passes at her. Knowing Jed and his brothers, Cade was sure they'd tested her but clearly, Mariah had managed to earn their respect.

Everything he learned about Mariah told him that she was a rare woman. And that made her dangerous. His mother had been such a woman—and his father had never recovered after losing her.

Cade had learned a hard lesson watching his father self-destruct—a wise man didn't get involved with a woman like Mariah. Because walking away wasn't an option—and losing her could plunge a man into a nightmare. It was true it had taken years for his dad to actually die—but Joseph Coulter had been a dead man walking from the second his wife died.

No sane man wanted that kind of dependence in his life, he thought grimly.

Cade spent a few more minutes with Jiggs before seeking his own bed, vowing to keep his distance from Mariah.

Two days later, Cade and J.T. spent all morning riding through brush and only netted three cows. The number of cattle the crew found had been dropping sharply and Cade was starting to believe it was time to head home with what they had. They could make a second sweep when they came back for the longhorns. He sent J.T. off to find the Turners and headed for Pete and Mariah's section.

He found Pete driving a small cluster of cattle toward the camp and corral, but Mariah wasn't with him. Cade rode closer and Pete lifted a hand in greeting.

"Where's Mariah?" Cade asked when he reached the older cowboy, scanning the empty prairie behind.

"She's just over that rise." Pete jerked his chin toward the hill on their right. "We found a calf wandering by itself and Mariah's walking it back, taking it slow. I told her I'd meet her at camp with this bunch." He nodded at the five cattle ahead of him.

"Is this all you've seen today?" Cade asked.

"Yep." Pete scanned the horizon before looking back at Cade. "You think maybe we've found all the strays we're goin' to, boss?"

"I'm leaning that direction," Cade replied. "J.T. and I drove in three head a bit ago. We've ridden over every acre of our section and I'm pretty sure we got them all. I sent J.T. out to check in with Jed and ask if he needs any help. Looks like you don't need another rider here so I'll look up Ash and Dallas. Could be it's time to head home and start branding."

Pete nodded. "I was thinkin' the same thing—told Mariah that when we stopped to eat lunch."

"Speaking of Mariah," Cade said as he swept a searching glance over the crest of the hill again but didn't see her. "I'll ride that way and check on her before I head over to Ash's section."

Pete nodded, lifting a hand in farewell as Cade reined Jiggs around and loped off.

Cade crested the hill, a long stretch of prairie spread out below him. Jiggs cantered down the slope and before they reached the base, Cade saw Mariah. She moved slowly toward him, her mare nudging a calf in the general direction of camp and corral.

As Cade watched, a cow broke out of a brush-filled coulee and trotted toward Mariah. The calf she'd been herding wasn't an orphan, Cade realized, and things were going to get very ugly, very fast.

Cade urged Jiggs into a full run and they raced toward Mariah as the calf bawled, answering his mother's call. The enraged cow bellowed, charging horse and rider, her head lowered, wicked hooked horns sweeping side to side as she ran.

Mariah fought to control her horse but the mare reared and spun, racing away from the charging cow.

Cade's blood ran cold. The cow stopped to nuzzle her calf, but Mariah was still in danger. The prairie was rough ground, filled with holes that could trip a horse. If Mariah's mare stepped in one of them, she could snap a leg and fall. Too many riders had died under just such circumstances and even if death didn't occur, broken bones were nearly guaranteed.

Uncaring for his own safety, Cade sent Jiggs running flat-out, the big horse stretching, reaching for more speed with each long stride, trying to catch the mare before there was an accident.

The powerful stallion closed the distance, the prairie a blur beneath his hooves as he ran. Mariah looked over her shoulder and saw them before she faced forward again, desperately trying to slow the mare. But Zelda fought the bit and barely slowed her headlong flight.

Jiggs drew alongside, the two horses racing neck and neck.

"Kick your feet free of the stirrups," Cade yelled.

Mariah complied instantly and he leaned toward her, controlling Jiggs with his knees and one hand on the reins.

His arm was an iron bar around her waist as he pulled

her from the saddle. She wrapped her arms around him, burying her face against the hard wall of his chest.

Mariah barely registered the pain in her ribs where Cade had gripped her. Cradled in his lap, the saddle-horn bruising her thigh, she knew Zelda kept running alongside Cade's big black. And then Jiggs slowed as Cade pulled him in with a powerful grip on the reins, and Mariah's terrified mare raced ahead on her own, empty stirrups slapping her sides.

Mariah shuddered, adrenaline pumping through her veins. She clenched fistfuls of Cade's shirt and pressed tighter against the warm hard strength of his body. Beneath her, Jiggs's run became a gallop, then a canter until at last he stood still, his sides heaving as he dragged in air and tossed his head.

Cade threw the reins over Jiggs's head, ground hitching the stallion, and slid off, taking Mariah with him and setting her on her feet.

She staggered as if the ground rolled under her, her legs impossibly wobbly, and Cade caught her by the arms, steadying her.

"Thank you," she managed to get out, pushing her tumbled hair out of her eyes. Her voice shook and so did her fingers, her breathing choppy. "I don't think I could have stopped Zelda."

"Are you all right?" he demanded, green eyes burning as he swiftly scanned her. His hands stroked down her arms as if checking for breaks.

"Yes…I think." She drew a deep breath, wincing as pain stabbed. Her ribs hurt where Cade had grabbed her to pull her off Zelda and she was sure she'd have bruises there tomorrow. "I'm fine."

"Don't lie to me." His voice was brusque. "You're in pain."

"I'll probably have a few bruises where you grabbed me," she admitted reluctantly.

"Damn it. I'm sorry." Cade ground out the words and let go of her arms, stalked several paces away, then strode back to loom over her. "What the hell were you doing with that calf? I told the entire crew to stay away from the longhorns."

Mariah stiffened. "How was I supposed to know it was a longhorn? Or that it wasn't an orphan?"

He ignored her comment. "You could have been killed. You're damn lucky you weren't hurt—if your mare had thrown you, that mama cow's horns would have ripped you to pieces."

"But she didn't." Mariah's temper flared. "I didn't do anything that any one of the crew wouldn't have done, given the circumstances."

"You're not anyone else in this crew," he roared. "I knew I shouldn't have let you come along on this trip. Chasing cows that are damn near feral is too dangerous for a woman."

"I wasn't chasing a longhorn." Mariah glared up at him, fists clenched at her sides. "And you're not being fair."

His jaw clenched, a muscle ticking. "You could have been killed," he repeated, as if the narrowness of her escape had shocked him.

"But I wasn't," Mariah said stubbornly. "And you wouldn't be yelling if this had happened to anyone else on the crew."

His eyes flared with heat and before Mariah could

blink, he wrapped his arms around her, hauled her up against his hard body, and took her mouth with his.

The kiss wasn't sweet, nor cajoling, nor slowly sensual. It was purely carnal and reeked of domination and desperation.

Mariah reeled under the instant surge of heat that flooded her but she fought the need to give in to the desire to meet lust with lust and struggled to get her hands between them to push at his chest. He was immovable. So she did the next best thing. She bit his lip.

His head jerked back and he swore.

"Dammit. What the hell was that for?" he demanded.

"*That* was to remind you caveman tactics don't work for me," she told him.

His eyes narrowed and a reluctant grin curved his mouth. "What does work for you?"

"You could ask. Nicely," she added.

One big hand left her waist to stroke up her spine, then down again with slow, sensual exploration. The slight pressure of his hand just below her waist nudged her tighter against his hips and the hard proof of his arousal.

"You want me to say please?" His deep voice rasped and his eyelids half-closed over eyes dark with sensual heat.

"That would be a step in the right direction," Mariah managed to say, her knees weak as he pressed her closer.

Green gaze holding hers, he bent and slowly stroked the tip of his tongue over the sensitive curve of her bottom lip, tasting her. "Please," he murmured.

It wasn't really a request, his voice more command than plea.

Mariah didn't care. She'd made a stand and now she only wanted more of his kisses. Her eyes drifted closed. "Yes," she whispered, going up on tiptoe to press her mouth against his.

What began with frustration quickly became much more. Mariah wrapped her arms around his neck, her fingers threading into the soft hair at his nape below his Stetson.

When at last he lifted his head and looked down at her, arousal streaked color across the high arch of his cheekbones and his eyes glittered with heat between thick black lashes. The sensual curve of his mouth drew her gaze, desire clenching low in her abdomen as she stared, wanting to feel his lips on hers again.

Then his eyes went opaque, his face wiped of expression, his mouth thinning as he stepped back.

"We'd better get back." His rough voice rasped, deeper, and the words were clipped.

He gathered Jiggs's reins and stepped into the saddle, holding out a hand to Mariah.

She was still disoriented, bemused by the suddenness of the last few minutes. Nevertheless, she took his hand and let him pull her up behind him. Without a word, Cade kneed Jiggs, lifting him into a canter.

Seated behind Cade, her arms wrapped around his waist, Mariah had too much time to think about that kiss on their way back to the camp. Stunned by the passion that had roared out of control between them, she couldn't make her mind function beyond the fact that no one had ever kissed her like that before.

Dangerous. He was dangerous to her peace of mind.

Too much heat. Her foolish body ached to have his mouth on hers again. She felt as if her nerve ends were singed, making her so sensitized that just touching him made her yearn to be wrapped against him.

After discussing the dwindling number of cows being found with the others over supper, Cade decided to start the drive back to the ranch the following morning. A part of Mariah eagerly looked forward to being home in her own cottage, soaking in the bathtub and sleeping in her own bed, but another part wished their time on the range wasn't over and she knew she'd always treasure the memory of the trip with Cade.

She and Pete helped herd the cattle the following morning as they moved them out of the corral and pointed them down the trail. The sun shone down, the dust rose from beneath the hooves of several hundred cattle and Mariah gladly rode Zelda on the far side of the herd, turning back any that tried to veer away from the main group.

Cade hailed her as the crew neared the flat where they'd parked the trucks.

"Mariah, I want you and Pete to ride ahead and drive my truck and his back to the ranch. You can trailer the horses with you. I'll send J.T. and the Turners to pick up the rest of the trucks after we get the herd home."

"All right."

She rode away with Pete, glancing to see Cade watching as they left the herd behind. They reached the flat and dismounted, loading their horses into the trailers. Pete drove out first, leaving Mariah to follow in Cade's big truck.

The seat was adjusted for Cade's long legs and Mariah

had to move it forward before she could reach the pedals. The truck was much newer than her little car and the dashboard looked like a cockpit, with gauges she didn't recognize. She'd ridden in the pickup as a passenger but that was very different from driving it.

She'd been apprehensive but once the big truck rolled forward, she stopped worrying. She lowered the windows and turned on the CD player. Instantly, the air was filled with bluegrass music. Surprised, Mariah smiled with delight. The song was one she recognized from her own CD of a Jerusalem Ridge appearance by Ralph Stanley and the Clinch Mountain Boys.

If she hadn't needed to pay close attention to the rough track she and Pete drove along, she would have loved to browse through the CD holder lying on the passenger seat.

Looking through a person's choice in music was as revealing as thumbing through their bookshelf, she thought with a smile.

The rest of the crew followed more slowly, trailing the herd of cattle.

Pete and Mariah arrived home well in advance of the riders herding the cattle. After they unloaded the horses and turned them out into the small corral, she walked to the cottage.

She dropped her duffel bag in the utility room next to the washing machine and walked straight to the bathroom where she stripped off every stitch of clothes and tossed them in the hamper. Then she turned on the water, waiting until it was warm before she stepped into the shower.

Access to an abundance of hot water was a luxury she'd come to appreciate over the last week, she thought, tipping her head back to let the water pour over her face and hair. She shampooed twice, the suds running in rivulets down her bare body, before she was satisfied. Then she repeated the process with floral bath gel before rinsing and stepping out onto the fluffy rug.

Drying off, she wrapped a towel around her hair and another around her body then padded back into her bedroom. The clothes hanging in her closet smelled like clean soap, without a trace of smoke from a campfire.

She held a sweater to her nose, breathing in the lovely scent.

I'm such a girl, she thought with a grin as she tossed the black sweater and a pair of jeans on the bed. And as she took a black lace bra and matching thong from the drawer to drop them atop the clothes, she couldn't help but think of Cade, her body heating as she remembered that kiss. Even now, she shied away from contemplating the searing passion that had engulfed them.

She dried her hair and applied makeup before dressing, stopping to toss a load of clothes in the washer before leaving the cabin. She walked back down the lane to the bunkhouse where Pete was already cutting up chicken to fry for dinner later.

"If you ever decide to retire from cowboying, Pete," she told him as she washed her hands, "you have a career ahead of you as a cook."

He flashed her a grin before returning his attention to the meat cleaver and the chopping block. "A good cowboy is automatically a good cook. Comes with the job."

Mariah laughed and took several bags of fresh vegetables from the fridge. They worked companionably side by side as they completed the prep work for dinner.

"What time do you think the herd will get here?" Mariah asked after they'd cleaned the kitchen and walked outside onto the porch. She searched the dirt trail that wound out of sight across the pasture but all was quiet.

"Hard to tell." Pete shrugged. "They'll get here when they get here." And with that, he stepped off the porch and headed for the machine shop, lifting a hand in good-bye as he went.

Mariah sighed and set off down the lane back to her cabin. She'd been happy when Cade assigned her to drive one of the trucks back. But now she almost wished she were riding drag behind the herd, participating in the final piece of the trip and spending more time with Cade.

It was late afternoon before the first cattle plodded into the home pasture, the rest of the herd soon spilling behind the leaders. Mariah was brushing Zelda in the horse corral when she heard the sound of several hundred hooves and the whistles and shouts of riders.

Pete emerged from the machine shop and hobbled across the ranch yard with surprising speed, climbing the corral fence for safety.

Mariah left Zelda and joined Pete for a better view, perching on the top rail to watch the stream of cattle pour through the open gate and into the paddock just past the barn. She narrowed her eyes and covered her nose with her forearm as dust rose, churned up beneath all the cattle's feet. The noise was deafening, calves bawling when some were separated from their mamas as the herd moved.

Cade, with Ash and Grady Turner, drove the young bulls into a separate enclosure and locked them in. They rode up to the corral where Pete perched with Mariah and scanned the herd of cows and calves inside the fence just beyond.

"What's the final head count, Cade?" Pete asked.

"Two hundred and fifty cows," Cade replied. "Nearly all of them have calves but I haven't counted how many are heifers or bull calves. And we rounded up a hundred and six young bulls that need to be cut."

"You plan to sell all hundred and six, or keep some for beef?" Pete asked.

Cade shrugged. "We could keep a steer or two to butcher, depending on how much room there is in the freezer."

"We could use at least one," Pete told him. "J.T. shot a deer last fall so there's venison but there's not much beef left."

Mariah kept her eyes firmly focused on the herd of cattle, purposely not looking at Cade. Just listening to his deep voice as he talked with Pete sent shivers rippling over her skin. She wondered if she was going to react to him like this from now on or if it would wear off in time.

The man could kiss beyond her wildest expectations. She'd been left shaken, stunned and unwilling to consider the meaning of the blaze of passion that had raged out of control between them.

"We'll start tomorrow. Jed and his brothers said they'd help brand and cut the bull calves."

Mariah realized the conversation between Cade, Pete and Jed had moved on to a discussion of the next stage with the cattle.

"If you want more help, there are a few local cowboys who'd be happy for the work," Pete put in.

"Hiring more hands would cut the time it takes to finish," Cade said. "The sooner we're done, the sooner we can sell the steers. Might be worth it."

Dallas and Grady rode up, with J.T. following and Mariah used the interruption to lean over and catch Pete's attention. "I'm going to start dinner at the bunkhouse," she told him. "Food should be ready in a half hour or so."

He nodded. "I'll tell the boys."

Mariah nodded and swung down from the corral fence, suppressing a smile at Pete's reference to Cade and the Turners as "boys." Although, she reflected as she walked quickly across the ranch yard and climbed the steps to the bunkhouse, Pete was at least seventy years old so it probably made sense that he thought of the men as *boys*.

She was carrying loaded bowls to the table when boots sounded on the porch outside. The quiet bunkhouse seemed to shrink in size as the seven men entered. They brought the scent of sage, campfire smoke and crisp Montana air with them, filling the room with deep male voices and laughter as they took turns washing off trail dust.

Mariah and Pete transferred huge platters and bowls of fried chicken, mashed potatoes and gravy, steamed carrots and broccoli from the kitchen area to the long table. Dallas and Grady were first to join the two and with faces and hands scrubbed clean, hair damp, they helped Mariah carry the last platters to the table.

The noise from voices, boots and chairs scraping on wood floors as everyone took seats gave way to silence as everyone ate. It wasn't until the hungry crew had filled their plates with second helpings that conversation grew from the occasional request to pass a bowl.

"I was thinking, Cade," Ash said. "Why don't we call the neighbors and ask if they want to come over to help brand? The Triple C hasn't had an old-fashioned roundup in years. I bet the Johnsons would get a kick out of being here and lending a hand. Same thing with the Petersens," he added, naming two families whose ranches shared fence lines with the Coulters.

"Ty and Mason will be here," Grady put in, naming his two remaining brothers. "Somebody had to stay home and take care of business but they sure weren't happy when they had to miss the roundup."

"That's the understatement of the year," Jed said drily. "They growled and stomped around for two days when they lost the toss and had to stay home. I'm sure they're planning to be here for branding. They'd probably be here tonight if they knew we were back."

"I'd hate to disappoint a Turner," Cade drawled. "And we can use the extra hands." He leaned back in his chair and sipped his coffee, his eyes narrowing in thought. "I remember the Petersen and Johnson families but not well. If you think they'd be willing to help, Ash, I'd be glad to have them."

"You'd better let Ben, Wayne and Asa know you're having a get-together," Pete put in. "Those three wouldn't want to miss it." He ran his hand over his white hair, his faded eyes twinkling. "Like me, they're old and stove-up, not good for much work, but we can hold down the corral fence and supervise."

"I'm sure you can, Pete," Cade said. "But I think you're wrong about being too old. You and Mariah ran in a fair share of the strays in that herd."

"True." Pete nodded with pride and looked across the table at Mariah. "What do you say, Mariah—want to sit on the fence with us four old cowboys and make sure the rest of these guys do the job right?"

Seated between J.T. and Grady Turner, Mariah glanced at Cade, noting the instant narrowing of his eyes as he focused on her with an intensity that made her shiver.

"No thanks, Pete," she said calmly, her gaze moving from Cade to Pete, then back to meet Cade's green stare. "I hate the smell of singed cowhide so if the boss doesn't mind, I'll skip the branding and spend my day doing women's work in the kitchen." She couldn't help a small smile when Cade winced at her words.

"You've earned the right to help with the branding if you want to, Mariah," he said, his deep voice neutral. "You did a great job last week."

Mariah shook her head, elation that he'd acknowledged her hard work flooding her. "Thanks, Cade, but I'll hang out in the kitchen. Actually," she said slowly as an idea occurred to her. "Maybe I'll talk to the neighbors, too, and see if the women want to come help. We could have an old-fashioned get-together, make it a party."

"Fine with me." Cade's agreement was quickly echoed by the rest of the men.

They lingered over coffee, discussing the next day's schedule, before finally pushing back their chairs. J.T. and Pete insisted on cleaning the kitchen, refusing to let her join them, and Mariah collected her jacket, calling good-night to the group.

"I'll walk you down to the cabin, Mariah." Dallas

helped her slip into her coat before taking his own jacket from a peg and shrugging into it.

"I need to talk to her." Cade's deep voice sounded behind her. "I'll walk her home."

Mariah glanced over her shoulder, her gaze meeting Cade's but she couldn't read his eyes.

She turned back to collect her hat and scarf from the peg where her coat had hung moments before. "Thanks for offering, Dallas."

He winked at her and grinned. "Maybe next time." He settled his Stetson over his brow and stepped out onto the porch.

Cade grabbed his own hat and coat and he and Mariah followed the general exodus from the bunkhouse. The Turners called good-night as they piled into the big cab of Jed's truck. The engine turned over with a throaty roar and as Mariah walked past the barn with Cade, the taillights glowed red as the truck drove away in the opposite direction toward the highway.

"They're good friends," Mariah said into the silence.

"Yeah, they are." Cade's voice rumbled with quiet agreement. "I've known them most of my life. Jed and I went to school together from kindergarten through high school."

"I've heard a lot of stories about them from people at the café," she said. "If even half of the stories are true, they've lived a…" She searched for the most diplomatic word. "Colorful life."

Cade's deep chuckle drifted on the quiet night air. "I'd say that's about right. You could have used a lot of words—like wild or crazy or hell-raisers, but they're good people."

"Someone at the café said their parents died when Jed was only fifteen. Is that true?"

Cade nodded. "Yeah, it's true. Jed's dad was a pilot—had a little Cessna, he loved to fly. Jed's mom went up with him when he was checking cattle one day and a storm blew in. No one really knows what happened but most folks believe lightning struck the plane. They crashed into Old Man Butte, about twenty miles south of town."

"That must have been terribly hard on the boys." Mariah couldn't imagine how the six young orphans had survived.

"It wasn't easy. Ned Anderson handled legal things but Jed took over running the ranch and hired a series of housekeepers to help with his younger brothers and keep the house together."

They reached the cabin and climbed the steps. Mariah paused, hand on the doorknob.

"You didn't tell me what you needed to talk to me about," she said, searching his face.

He stared down at her, the silence growing. "I wanted to know if you're all right," he said finally. He moved closer, brushing his fingertips over her cheek.

"If I'm all right?" Confused, Mariah gazed up at him. His touch was warm, gentle. "I don't know what you mean."

"I grabbed you too hard when I pulled you off your mare yesterday. You said you'd have bruises. Do your ribs still hurt?"

"Oh, that," Mariah said with relief. "I'm fine."

"I'm sorry," he said gruffly. "I didn't think about whether I was holding you too tight."

"Please, don't worry about it. I'm sure I've had worse bruises from carrying heavy trays at the café."

He tucked a strand of hair behind her ear and frowned. "You get bruised at work?"

"Not often," she hastened to assure him. "It's only happened a couple of times when I wasn't paying attention and walked into the doorjamb between the dining room and the kitchen with a loaded tray."

"Your boss ought to pad the damn doorjamb—or better yet, carry the heavy trays himself."

Mariah felt her eyes widen and she smiled softly, secretly pleased by his obvious concern on her behalf. "I don't mind, it's all part of the job. And if I'd been paying closer attention to what I was doing, I wouldn't have bumped into the doorjamb."

He looked unconvinced. "Speaking of the café, when do you have to go back to work?"

"Not for several days. Sally told me to take as much time as I needed so I'll go back when the branding is over."

"All right. Let me know if you need supplies. The number of men on the crew seems to be growing by the hour. Are you sure you're okay with feeding everybody?"

"Yes, absolutely. I'll call in friends to help—we'll have fun doing it."

"All right." He hesitated, staring down at her.

For one heart-stopping, aching moment, Mariah was certain he was going to kiss her.

But then he touched the brim of his hat, murmured good-night and strode off down the lane toward the house.

Disappointed, she turned and went inside, closing the door with more than her usual firmness.

She was annoyed with herself for regretting their good-night hadn't included another of those bone-melting kisses.

Chapter Nine

"I'm glad you called and asked us to help, Mariah," Sally McKinstry beamed. "I haven't been to a neighborhood roundup like this in...well, simply ages."

Mariah perched next to Sally on the top rail of the horse corral. A dozen dusty pickup trucks were parked near the ranch house; beyond the barn, two older men in boots and hats were feeding wood to a branding fire while horses and riders moved cattle through a chute, one by one.

Just to the left of the bunkhouse, close enough to easily access the kitchen, several men and women clustered around a spit where beef turned slowly. The aroma of barbecuing beef drifted to where the two women sat.

"I'm glad you could come out—and I can hardly believe Ed left Mac and Julie to run the café." Mariah glanced at the group near the bunkhouse where Ed's bulky figure stood out among the crowd.

"He went to the café at four a.m. to make cinnamon rolls," Sally assured her. "But he told me there was no way he'd miss being here."

Mariah laughed. "Well, trust me, everyone will appreciate his effort. The smell of the barbecue is already making me hungry." She skimmed the ranch yard, unconsciously searching for Cade in the hive of activity. She found him with the branding crew near the fire. He'd shed his coat and worked in his shirtsleeves, wielding a branding iron with efficiency. As she watched, he lifted his head, laughing at a comment from a young cowboy holding the calf. "It's wonderful that all Joseph's neighbors have turned out to help his son," she said softly.

"They would have helped Joseph, too, if he would have let them." Sally laid a comforting hand on Mariah's.

"I know." Mariah had always known that Joseph's isolation from the world of Indian Springs had been of his own choosing. Over the years, his neighbors had apparently come to accept and respect his wish to be left alone. "We—Pete, J.T. and myself—helped Joseph with a much smaller version of this each year. But we never had this many cattle and of course, since we branded more often, we didn't have to handle any cattle this age and size."

"Cade and the Turners don't seem to be having any trouble," Sally commented.

The words had barely left her mouth when a cow tried to escape the riders separating her from her calf and for a few minutes, dust stirred, men yelled, cows bawled and the noise was deafening. As quickly as it rose, however, it subsided as the riders shoved the cow back into the herd.

"Well, not too much trouble, anyway," Mariah said drily.

"Nothing they can't handle," Sally said cheerfully. "I need to go check in with Ed and see if he needs any help with the food."

"I'll come with you." Mariah climbed down from the top rail and the two women skirted the working men on their way to the bunkhouse.

"Carrie Petersen mentioned that Cade gave her and her friends permission to have an end-of-work party in the barn loft tonight," Sally said as they walked.

"J.T. mentioned that earlier this morning," Mariah said. She was delighted Cade had agreed to the teenager's request and she enjoyed seeing the Triple C come alive with neighbors having a good time. Surely having his neighbors and friends rally round to help him was a powerful reminder to Cade that the Coulters belonged on the Triple C.

Later that evening, after the last calf had been branded and the barbecue pronounced a rousing success, the five piece band of local musicians set up in the barn loft and began to play.

Mariah went to her cabin to shower and change clothes and an hour later, left her cabin to walk quickly back down the lane. The sound of music, laughter and the pound of her neighbors' and friends' feet against floor boards as they gathered in the loft of the big barn grew louder as she neared. Carrying the black pumps she'd chosen to wear with a black wool skirt and pale blue cashmere sweater, she neared the bright square of light that poured from the open door.

A group of people clustered just outside called hellos as she approached and she returned their greetings, recognizing several of the teenagers in the crowd.

She stepped inside and carried her coat to the tack room, laying it over a saddle seat already piled high with jackets, coats and scarves. She tugged off her winter boots and slipped her feet into the high-heeled black pumps before smoothing her palms down the black wool over her hips. She tugged the hem of her sweater and straightened it before realizing she was nervous, purposely delaying going upstairs.

This was the first time she would see Cade in a purely social setting and she had no idea whether he would ignore her, treat her like one of the crew, or follow through on the promise of the heat in each glance he'd sent her since that kiss.

Regardless, she told herself with determination, she'd never been nervous about attending social functions at Indian Creek and she didn't plan to start now.

She squared her shoulders, lifted her chin, and turned on her heel, leaving the tack room.

"Hey, Mariah!"

Julie's call halted her just as she reached the second wide plank of the loft stairs. Mariah looked over her shoulder and smiled at her friend and her husband just inside the doorway.

"Hi, Julie. You can drop your coats in the tack room—I'll wait for you."

"Great." Julie caught her husband's arm and tugged him with her. Moments later, they returned and joined Mariah on the stairs. "I'm so glad you called about the party. We were going to watch an old movie on TV tonight and this is so much more fun, isn't it, Bob?"

Julie's husband nodded, his eyes twinkling with affection as his gaze scanned his wife's animated expression. "Much more fun," he echoed. "Unless she tries to make me dance the tango," he told Mariah with a straight face. "I don't do the tango."

Julie rolled her eyes. "Neither do I, so I think you're safe."

They reached the top of the stairs and paused, looking over the big crowded space beneath the barn rafters.

"Wow." Julie's delight was heartfelt.

"Definitely wow," Mariah responded. The teenagers had worked all afternoon, cleaning, sweeping, organizing, and the space looked great. They'd hung up bright wool blankets around the room and created a foot-high stage at one end where the band played. The wide-planked floor had been swept clean and bales of straw were arranged around the sides for guests to sit on. Sawhorses with boards laid across them and covered with sheets created tables along one wall where drinks and snacks were set out. The makeshift tables were also set up at intervals around the edge of the room and most of the folding chairs were filled with guests. "They've done an incredible job. I hardly recognize the loft."

Julie nodded and opened her mouth to reply but was interrupted by Sally shouting her name.

The three scanned the crowded room and located Sally, standing on the far side of the room, waving at them. Mariah lifted a hand to let her know they'd seen her and the three threaded their way around groups of people. The center of the room was thronged with dancers, shifting and swaying to the fast beat of a Kenny Chesney tune.

"Hi, you two." The trio reached Sally and Ed, taking seats at the rough table. "How did you manage to save us seats? This place is crazy crowded." Julie set her small purse on the table and lifted Sally's glass to sniff. "What are you drinking?"

"It's just punch."

Mariah laughed at Julie's raised eyebrows. "We couldn't serve alcohol, Julie, not without a license. But anyone who wants to can bring their own."

"Did you know that, Bob?" Julie asked her husband.

"Yes, honey, I did." He took a small bottle of rum from his coat pocket.

"This is only one of the reasons I adore you." She beamed with delight and gave him a quick kiss.

Mariah laughed at the smug satisfaction on Bob's face. "You know her so well," she said.

"That's what makes a good husband," he said with conviction.

"Is that true, Ed?"

"Absolutely." Ed leaned over, making a smacking noise as he kissed Sally's cheek.

As the couples bantered, Mariah felt a twist of wistful longing. Being part of a couple always seemed so attractive when she was around these four, because they were so comfortable with each other and open about their deep affection.

She couldn't help but wonder if she'd ever have that level of intimacy with anyone.

"Hey, Mariah, wanna dance?"

She looked up and saw J.T. He held out his hand and

when she hesitated, he caught her fingers in his and pulled her up out of her chair.

"J.T., I'm not sure I know how to dance to this," she protested as he drew her onto the floor, tugging her along behind him. The music had a fast beat and couples spun and moved to the rhythm.

"I'll teach you," he told her with a grin. "It's easy."

By the time the song ended, she was out of breath, flushed and exuberant, blood pumping faster through her veins.

"This is fun." She had to lean in to shout into J.T.'s ear because the dancers were shouting and stomping their feet, encouraging the band to repeat the song.

From behind her, a warm hand settled over the curve of her shoulder. Before Cade spoke, the shiver that spread from his hand and through her body told her who stood there.

Cade saw Mariah the moment she stepped into the room. Leaning against a support post at the far end of the big loft, he'd been watching the stairway for the last half hour and growing increasingly impatient.

The wait was worth it, he thought. Mariah's hair was loose, brushing her shoulders and gleaming silver against her pale blue sweater. The sweater had a modest scoop neck and clung to the curve of her breasts, the long sleeves covering her to her wrists. A black skirt smoothed over her hips, following the curve of thigh to just below her knee but when she moved, a side slit parted to reveal, then conceal, a flash of smooth knee and thigh. She wore black high heels and Cade would have bet she thought the outfit was conservative.

She was wrong.

The blue sweater and black skirt covered her from shoulder to knee but it only made him want to peel them off her and explore the curves they clung to. And the flash of thigh made him want to stroke his palm up her leg to test just how soft her skin was beneath the fabric.

She lingered with another couple just past the top of the stairway, scanning the room for a few moments. Then they disappeared into the crowd. Cade caught glimpses of Mariah's silvery hair as the three wove their way around people to join Sally and Ed McKinstry at a table. They'd barely sat down before J.T. drew Mariah out onto the dance floor.

When the music stopped, Cade joined them.

"Can I cut in?"

Mariah turned her head and saw Cade nod at J.T., his gaze hooded.

"Sure, boss." J.T. stepped back, disappearing into the crowd before Mariah could protest.

The opening bars of a slow George Strait song quieted the crowd and Cade's hand left her shoulder, stroking down her arm in an easy caress before settling on her waist. He turned her into his arms and she automatically slipped her hand into his, the other resting on his shoulder.

The powerful muscles of his arm flexed, shifting subtly beneath her hand as he drew her nearer and swept her into the dance steps.

Mariah closed her eyes and took in the faint spicy scent of his aftershave blended with the clean smell of soap, underlaid with a scent that was uniquely Cade himself. She felt surrounded by him—one arm around her waist, the other enclosing hers while his tall, broad body created a wall between her and the rest of the crowd on the dance floor.

"I wanted to thank you for organizing your friends and the neighbors," he murmured against her hair. "It must have taken a lot of time and effort to plan all of this."

"Everyone was happy to help," Mariah replied, tilting her head back to meet his gaze. "They're all glad to see you return to the Triple C and making the ranch come alive again—it's such a good thing for the community."

"Yeah?" One dark eyebrow quirked, his green eyes skeptical. "I wonder if they'll feel the same if we have to sell the place to pay the taxes."

"I hope that doesn't happen," she said gravely. "And I don't see you letting it happen without a fight."

"No, not without a fight," he agreed. "But there's no guarantee this is a battle we can win."

"But you're trying," she replied with conviction. "I think the community turning out to help over the last few days is their way of saying they're hoping you win— and stay in Montana."

"You really think Indian Springs wants my brothers and me in the county? Despite all the crazy stuff we did when we were growing up here?" His eyes smiled, teasing her.

"Absolutely," she said firmly.

"And how about you?" His arm tightened fractionally, urging her closer until her body was pressed to his from breast to thigh. "Do you want Coulters to stay on the Triple C?"

Her nipples beaded, breasts gently crushed against the hard muscles of his chest. Each step they took to the

slow music moved her thighs against his, shifted her
hips against his, and her body felt as if it was on nuclear
meltdown. She slicked her tongue across lips gone dry
and his eyes narrowed, turning to hot dark emerald as
he followed the movement.

"I'll take that as a yes." His voice rasped, roughened.

Mariah realized he was struggling with the same
desire that tortured her. She wished they were anywhere
but here, surrounded by the crowd.

His eyes flared with awareness and she knew her
expression must have reflected her wish for privacy.

Cade stopped dancing, caught her hand and drew her
with him into a shadowed corner, where a thick roof-
support post sheltered them from the crowd. His gaze
held hers as he backed her against the wool Pendleton
blanket hung over the rough wall, planted his forearm
on the wall and leaned closer.

"I haven't been able to forget that kiss," he murmured, nuzzling the soft skin of her throat just below
her ear. "In fact, I've been dreaming about it." His free
hand slipped around her waist. "I keep wondering if it
could have been as good as I remember." He lifted his
head a fraction and looked down at her. "What do you
think?"

"I think…we should try it again and find out."

His eyes darkened with heat and his mouth curved
in a sensual half smile. "Yeah, maybe we should."

He lowered his head, his mouth taking hers with slow,
coaxing persuasion.

The sensitive nerves just under her skin awakened,
stirring awareness and unfurling tendrils of heat.

She slid her palms up his chest, over warm hard

muscles and the solid curve of his shoulders, to wrap her arms around his neck. Her fingertips met the thick silk of his hair at his nape.

There was no sense of time or awareness of the crowd beyond the corner where they stood. There was only his mouth on hers, the press of his body against hers as heat and arousal, desire and need, roared to life between them.

"Come to the house with me," he whispered, lifting his head at last, his lips moving against the shell of her ear.

"We can't. This is your party—you're the host. You can't leave this early."

He lifted his head just far enough to look into her eyes. "Later?"

Her lashes lowered, her heart beating so fast the thunder was loud in her ears. "Maybe. At my place."

"I don't care whose place—just don't keep me wondering for an hour. If I have to stay and play nice, tell me yes."

"Are we bargaining here?"

A slow smile curved his mouth. "No. I'm begging you not to tease me. I'm on the edge already."

"Then the answer is yes." She was done teasing, too. And now that the decision was made, anticipation curled through her body but her nerves seemed to settle, as if knowing how the night would end had temporarily calmed them. She ducked under his arm just as his hands tightened to pull her close. "But in the meantime, a good host should circulate."

He caught her hand and pulled it through the crook of his arm, covering it with his warm palm to keep it on his forearm. "I'll play the good host if you'll be the hostess."

"All right."

"First let's get some food, I'm hungry."

They left the shelter of the corner, wending their way around the edge of the dance floor to reach the make-shift tables against the far wall.

Cade handed Mariah a plate and picked up one for himself, hesitating as he looked at the dozens of bowls and platters arranged down the long table. "Any suggestions?"

"Sally made the fried chicken, Ed baked the six-tier German chocolate cake, and Mrs. Petersen brought the potato salad." Mariah pointed to the items as she listed them. "Don't miss any of them, or you'll regret it." She scanned the table. "Actually, you should try everything—Indian Springs has a lot of great cooks and most of them are here tonight."

"You want me to try everything?" Cade shook his head. "Honey, if I do that, I won't be able to move for two days."

She laughed. "All right, maybe you need to pace your-self." She picked up a piece of Sally's crunchy chicken. "Shall we join Ed and Sally, Julie and Bob when we're done here? They have a table on the other side of the loft."

"Sure." Cade looked down at his nearly full plate. "We're going to need somewhere to put these plates."

He snagged two bottles of beer from a tub filled with ice. "Lead the way."

He followed her around the perimeter of the loft.

"Hey, Mariah," Julie called as they neared. "We were just wondering where you'd disappeared."

"I was dancing with Cade." Mariah set down her plate and sat, catching Cade's arm to pull him down beside her. "I think you all know Joseph's son, Cade, don't you?"

Sally and Julie smiled hello, while Ed and Bob leaned across the table to shake hands.

"Great party, Cade," Julie said.

"Thanks." He smiled and looked at Mariah. "All the credit goes to Mariah and her friends. I didn't have much to do with it."

"You gave us a reason to have a party when you scheduled the branding."

He shrugged, his smile wry. "That's not much of a contribution."

"Did you brand enough steers to make the roundup worthwhile?" Bob asked.

"I can always use more but to be honest, I was very surprised at the final total. Pleasantly surprised," he added.

"Have you got a buyer?" Ed asked. "Because if you haven't sold the lot, I'd like to buy a few to butcher for beef for the café. I bet the owners of the Black Bear would take some, too."

"Of course, they would." Sally winked at Cade. "That's prime free range beef you're holding in your corrals, Cade. I wouldn't be surprised if you could get double or triple the normal price if you contacted a broker."

"That's a brilliant idea, Sally." Mariah beamed at her friend. "Restaurants in Denver feature free range beef on menus and it's always more expensive."

"Thanks for the tip, Sally," Cade told her. "I'll look

into it. And Ed, we'll cut out steers for you and any other Indian Springs restaurants that are interested."

"Great." A smile lit Ed's craggy features. "As a matter of fact, as soon as you're finished with that," he said as he pointed at Cade's full plate, "we'll go find Denise Larson—her and her brother own the Black Bear. I saw her dancing a bit ago and there's no time like the present to get a deal worked out."

"Ed," Sally protested. "You promised no business tonight."

He patted her arm. "Honey, this is just a little friendly dealing between friends, right, Cade?"

Cade grinned, white teeth flashing in his tan face. "Right, Ed."

A half hour later, after emptying their plates, Cade, Ed and Bob excused themselves to find Denise Larson and her brother.

Julie heaved a dramatic sigh as the three women watched the men walk away. "Mariah, that man is so gorgeous."

"Yes, he is." Mariah's pleased satisfaction made the other two laugh out loud.

"Ed hasn't looked at me like that for years," Sally told her with a sigh.

"Like what?" Mariah asked, lifting her bottle to drink.

"Like you're a big bowl of ice cream and he wants to lick you all over." Julie's smile was wicked.

Mariah sputtered and choked. "Julie!" She wiped moisture from her hand and stared at her friend.

Julie's smile was wide. "Well, he does." She turned to Sally. "Doesn't he?"

Sally nodded emphatically, her eyes gleaming with laughter. "Oh, yes. He definitely does."

Mariah didn't know what to say. She was delighted that Cade wasn't hiding his interest but on the other hand, she wasn't sure exactly how their attraction for each other would turn out.

Sally leaned over and patted her hand. "Relax and enjoy it, Mariah. I remember when Ed and I first got together and he had that look in his eye. We had *so* much fun."

"You two are incorrigible," Mariah told them.

"No we're not," Julie protested. "This is basic Married 101 class. Take notes, because given the way Cade looks at you, I'm guessing you're going to need this important info."

"We aren't even dating," Mariah protested.

"You haven't had time," Sally pointed out reasonably. "He's too busy trying to save the Triple C and find his brothers."

"And you're too busy helping him," Julie added.

"You don't think we should at least go to a movie or something before…" Mariah waved a hand vaguely.

"No." Sally and Julie chorused.

"You have the rest of your life to date," Sally told her. "Besides, the two of you have probably spent more hours together than a couple who's dated for a year."

She was right, Mariah realized. She and Cade had spent hours and hours together over the last weeks, bonded by working toward common goals on the Triple C.

Before she could pursue Sally's comment further, the men returned and conversation veered into more conventional channels.

Mariah and Cade danced, chatted with neighbors, rejoined Sally, Ed, Julie and Bob for a drink before moving on, and all the time, the simmering sexual awareness between them grew steadily stronger, hotter.

At last the crowd began to thin, guests making a point of stopping to thank Cade for his hospitality. After a half hour of goodbyes, Cade excused himself and Mariah saw him stop Pete, the two exchanging words before Cade returned.

"Pete's going to play host with Asa, Ben and Wayne for the rest of the night," he told her, slipping his arm around her waist and walking her toward the stairs. "Let's get our coats and I'll walk you home."

Mariah murmured an assent and went with him, anticipation ratcheting higher with each step as they left the barn and walked down the lane to her cabin. His hand was warm around hers and they climbed the steps without a word. Inside, he slipped her coat from her shoulders, shrugged out of his, and tossed them on the chair just inside the door. Then he knelt to take off her boots.

Mariah balanced herself with one hand on his shoulder, the muscles flexing and bunching beneath her fingertips as he removed first one, then the other of her boots. When he stood, he rested his hands on her waist and looked down at her.

"If you've changed your mind about this, tell me now," he said, his deep voice a low rumble in the quiet house.

"No, I haven't changed my mind." She slipped her hand in his and tugged, drawing him down the hall to her bedroom.

She'd left a lamp burning on the nightstand, the linens turned back invitingly.

"Were you expecting company?"

"What?" Startled, she looked up and met his gaze, his green eyes unreadable. "No, I always leave a light on and the covers turned down when I go out at night. I hate coming home to a dark house."

The hard lines of his face eased. "Good to know." He slipped his arms around her waist and tugged her near until her hips and thighs rested against his. "I'm glad you weren't expecting company tonight." He bent and brushed a kiss against her mouth. "Unless it was me."

"I, um…" Mariah lost track of what she was about to say when he brushed another teasing kiss at the corner of her mouth. "I don't bring men home, Cade."

He went still, his mouth leaving its warm exploration of the sensitive skin just below her ear as he lifted his head. His gaze searched hers. "Never?"

"Never here. Never since I came to Indian Springs."

"Then it's been a while for you," he murmured. "We'll take it slow."

"I'm not sure I want slow," she confessed.

A slow, sensual smile curved his mouth. "I'm not sure I can give you slow, but I'm willing to try."

Before Mariah could reply, his mouth took hers and all thoughts of slow, leisurely lovemaking went up in a blaze of heat. She moaned in protest when Cade's lips left hers. He leaned back, caught the hem of her sweater and pulled it up and off, dropping it on the floor. His gaze fastened on the curve of her breasts, covered in pale blue silk and lace, and she felt the flick of green fire before he gently turned her around.

He made short work of her bra, his palms smoothing up her back and over her shoulders to push the scrap of satin and lace off her body. It fell to the floor but Mariah barely noticed because Cade pulled her against him, his hands surrounding her to cup the sensitive fullness of her breasts.

His lips found the place where shoulder met throat and she felt the scrape of his teeth, his mouth hot as he marked her. Mariah arched back against him, lost in sensation.

He muttered an oath and released her to unzip her skirt and push it down over her hips, leaving her clad only in blue silk and lace thong and thigh high stockings. He spun her around, wrapped his arms around her waist and nudged her backward until the backs of her knees hit the edge of the mattress.

"You're wearing too many clothes," she told him, tugging at the snaps of his shirt. The fasteners gave way with audible pops as she pulled his shirt open down to his waistband. She had to unbuckle his belt and undo the top button of his jeans before she could tug his shirt free. She laid her flat hands against the washboard muscles of his abdomen and slid them upward, pushing the shirt aside. Distracted by the hard male body under her palms, she leaned into him, her bare breasts cushioned against his chest, and pressed an openmouthed kiss to the throbbing pulse at the base of his throat.

He growled, arms tightening as he pressed her closer, and the pulse beneath her mouth pounded harder.

"Enough," he groaned. He eased her away from him and laid her on the bed before stripping off his shirt. He bent to yank off his boots, then shoved his jeans and shorts down his long legs and kicked them aside.

Mariah's mouth went dry. He was an intimidating man fully clothed. Naked, he was breathtaking. Barely knowing she did so, she scooted over on the bed, widening the space between them.

Cade didn't give her time to worry. He bent over her, pressing a deep kiss against her navel before he tugged her panties down her legs. Too impatient to take time to remove her stockings, his mouth covered hers with carnal demand that quickly swamped any second thoughts on Mariah's part.

She wrapped her arms around his neck and urged him closer, reveling in the heat as his muscled body lowered over hers.

The cove of her hips cradled the hard angles of his, his powerful thighs between hers. Drowning in sensation, Mariah ran her hands down the length of his spine and wrapped her legs around his hips, murmuring an incoherent demand.

Cade's hand closed over her thigh, hips flexing as he joined them with one controlled thrust.

Mariah stiffened, adjusting to the intrusion, but then he moved, stroking her, pulling her with him into an ocean of sensation and desire that burned higher until they came apart together, exploding into a thousand brilliant pieces.

She fell asleep in Cade's arms, her arms around his waist, her head on his shoulder. Sometime later, she woke to find him nuzzling her throat, his hands moving with tactile enjoyment over her back.

"Mmm," she murmured. "Is it morning?"

"No, not even close."

"Good." She stroked her hands down the hard line of

his spine. His muscles rippled in reaction to her touch, his skin like satin over steel.

He kissed her throat, the underside of her chin, then the soft skin below her ear. Mariah shuddered, turning more fully in his arms until more of her bare skin pressed against as much of his as she could manage.

He responded by sliding his hands down her back to cup her bottom and press her closer.

Mariah murmured her approval and tugged his face higher until she could press her lips to his. Instantly, languid teasing became hotter, focused and intense, and his weight pinned her to the bed as he moved between her thighs.

She thought hazily how wonderful it was that their bodies seemed so perfectly attuned before she was swept away.

Chapter Ten

They spent the night making love, Cade waking her again just before dawn lightened the dark sky outside her bedroom window.

"I wish you didn't have to go," Mariah said, wrapping her arms around his waist as he poured coffee in the kitchen. He was dressed while she wore only a light robe.

"I have to." He turned, his mouth meeting hers in a slow, thorough kiss before he stepped back to pick up a filled mug and hand it to her. "I don't want you to worry about Pete and J.T. seeing me leave your house this early."

"Mmm." Mariah sipped her coffee, knowing she would be more comfortable if their night together was private.

Cade leaned his hips against the counter behind him

and sipped his coffee, his gaze warm as it skated over her. He glanced around the kitchen with its touches of blue and yellow in the pottery on the sideboard, the place mats on the pine table and canisters on the white tiled countertop.

"I like what you've done with this place," he told her. "Looks a lot better than I remember it from the last time I was here, years ago."

"Thank you." Mariah felt a surge of pleasure at his words, her gaze touching lightly on the sunny kitchen. "I'm glad you're okay with Joseph leaving it to me."

"Hey." He shrugged. "I don't blame you for wanting a home. Especially after you told me your mom and dad are gone and the house you grew up in was sold. Everybody needs a place that belongs to them."

Something about his comment didn't feel right to Mariah.

"You mean you don't blame Joseph any longer for leaving me the cabin?"

"I don't blame any man for giving you anything," he told her with a half grin. "If you asked me for every acre of the Triple C, I'd be tempted to hand it over, just for one of your smiles."

The apprehension in her stomach grew stronger.

"You still believe I used my friendship with your father to get him to leave me the cabin, don't you?" she whispered, numb with hurt.

"I didn't say that. I don't know why my dad left you the cabin."

"But you think I influenced him in some way." Mariah clenched the mug, willing him to unequivocally deny her statement.

"Honey, every beautiful woman influences every man who comes in contact with her."

"We aren't talking about every other woman. I specifically want to know if you still believe I somehow convinced Joseph to leave me this cabin."

The small silence stretched between them, his green gaze holding hers. "I don't know what happened between you and my father," he said at last. "What I do know is that he held on to the rest of the Triple C and apparently damn near starved doing it. Given that, why would he give up a cabin and land?" He shrugged again. "I don't have the answer to that."

Mariah fought back tears of hurt and anger, swallowing twice before she could speak past the thick emotion lodged in her throat. "I'd like you to leave, Cade. If you don't know by now that I would never purposely use Joseph, then you don't know me at all."

He stiffened, eyes narrowing over her. "I didn't say you purposely used Joseph. And after what happened between us last night, I'd say I know you more than a little."

"A physical relationship isn't enough for me—and without trust, that's all we'll ever have." Mariah struggled to keep her voice from trembling. "I want more than just great sex."

"Just great sex," he repeated, his voice rough. "You think that's all this is?"

"I don't know. And," she told him, fighting back tears, "neither of us will ever have a chance to find out. There isn't a future for us. I can't be with a man who doesn't trust me." She paused, dragging in a breath through lungs that felt crushed with the pain in her chest. "I won't be working on the ranch any longer," she told him.

"Are you telling me you're quitting?"

"Yes."

His eyes flared, his mouth setting in a hard line. "Mariah, don't do this."

"I don't see that I have a choice. Unless you can tell me, truthfully, that I'm wrong."

"Dammit, Mariah, this isn't personal. If you were a saint, I'd still assume there was a part of you, whether you know it or not, that looks out for number one. Every human does it. I'm not saying I blame you—and I'm not saying I even care anymore. You're here—I'm here—we're great in bed together and the reasons Dad left you the cabin don't necessarily matter all that much anymore. Not to me."

"But they do to me," she said softly, tears hovering on her lashes. "It matters a great deal to me that you believe I acted without honor."

Cade thrust his fingers through his hair, raking it back off his brow in frustration. "When did I ever say you're not an honorable person?" he demanded.

"If I was kind to Joseph in order to get a piece of his estate, then I acted dishonorably."

"Hell." He stared at her, clearly frustrated.

"We can't get past it," she said quietly.

"Is it this important to you?"

"Yes."

"Important enough to walk away from what we could have here?"

"Yes." Her voice throbbed, husky with tears.

His hands settled on the curve of her shoulders and he pulled her forward, wrapping his arms around her as he bent his head and took her mouth in a fierce, hard kiss. When he set her away from him, her knees were unsteady.

"All right, I have to respect your decision," he bit out, a muscle flexing along his jawline. "But if you change your mind, you know where to find me."

And he turned and walked out, the door closing behind him with a loud snap.

Mariah held herself erect, stiff, until she heard the door close before bending at the waist, keening with grief. She staggered into the living room and fell onto the sofa, muffling her sobs against the cushions. She didn't know how long she cried before the tears slowed. Exhausted, she pulled the afghan off the back of the sofa and curled under it. She couldn't go back to bed. Cade's scent was all over the sheets and blanket. She couldn't bear to know he'd never share the bed with her again.

Cade stood in his kitchen, waiting for the coffee to finish brewing, and watched Mariah's car move down the lane, past his house, and onward to cross the bridge and head for the highway.

He glanced at the clock. *She must be working the early shift today,* he thought.

In the five days since they'd made love, she'd refused to speak to him. He'd called but she didn't answer her phone. He'd walked down the lane and knocked on her door but if she heard him, she wouldn't open the door.

She'd told him that she didn't want to see him again. Apparently, he thought with frustration, she'd meant it.

Hell, he thought with disgust. *This is what happens*

when a man gets hung up on a woman. Can't stop thinking about her, bothered when she won't talk to me.

He'd grown accustomed to having her in his life, seeing her every night over dinner at the bunkhouse and dammit, he missed her.

More than that, he was miserable without her.

He filled an insulated travel mug with coffee and left the kitchen, pausing at the door to shrug into his coat and settle his hat on his head before going outside. Across the ranch yard, the windows of the bunkhouse gleamed with welcoming light and Cade stalked toward it. With luck, Pete had breakfast already cooking on the stove.

The aroma of frying bacon hit his nostrils the minute he pulled open the door. J.T. stepped out of the bathroom, his hair wet from the shower, a cloud of warm steamy air following him.

"Morning, boss." Pete stood at the stove, a white chef's apron tied around his waist. "Eggs are on, coffee's on the table."

"Thanks." Cade shrugged out of his coat and hung it on a hook along with his hat. He set his insulated mug on the table and went into the kitchen, dropping slices of bread into the toaster before he set the butter dish and utensils atop three plates and carried the stack back to the table.

"I'll bring the toast, Cade," J.T. told him.

Cade set plates and utensils at three places before pulling out a chair. He emptied the coffee from his insulated mug in one long swallow and refilled it from the carafe as J.T. and Pete slid platters of food onto the table.

The three ate almost silently until their plates were emptied.

"What's on the schedule today, boss?" Pete asked when they'd all refilled cups and sat back.

"I'm going to round up the longhorns and drive them in. The Turners volunteered to help—they're bringing the mules with the boxes already packed. I want you two to stay here and keep an eye on things while I'm gone," Cade said.

"Are you sure you couldn't use another hand?" J.T. asked. "I'd rather chase longhorns than take a biology test today."

"Sorry, J.T., but I can't do it. You missed too much class time with the last roundup. I don't see the principal giving me permission to take you out of school again so soon." Cade couldn't help but be amused by the teenager's grimace of disappointment.

"How long do you think you'll be gone?" Pete asked.

"I'm not sure, a few days at least."

"J.T. and I'll keep things ticking over here. Anything in particular you want done?" Pete leaned forward to pick up the carafe of coffee and refill his mug.

"There are several cows that were bred late and look ready to drop calves any day—in both the home pasture herd and the cattle we drove here from the outer pasture. Keep an eye on them—we need every calf we can save."

Pete nodded. "Will do."

"If we have any trouble, I'm sure Mariah will help," J.T. put in. "She always took care of the babies for Joseph so she knows the mama cow's calving history better than anyone else. And she told me last night that she's working the afternoon shift starting tomorrow so I won't feel guilty if I have to wake her up in the middle of the night."

Cade wanted to ask J.T. how Mariah was doing, since the teenager had obviously seen her the evening before, but kept his mouth shut.

"Good to hear she's working a later shift," Pete put in. "She's been pulling double shifts for almost a week. She works too hard but when I told her so, she just laughed at me."

"She laughed?" J.T.'s brows lifted in surprise. "Man, I haven't heard her laugh in days."

"Well, it wasn't much of a laugh," Pete said with slow deliberation. His shrewd blue gaze pinned Cade. "I get the impression somethin's upset her lately."

Cade didn't rise to the bait. Instead, he carefully blanked his expression and met the old cowboy's gaze without commenting.

"Damn." J.T. glanced at his watch and shot out of his chair. "Look at the time—and I haven't fed the horses yet. If I don't hurry up, I'll miss catching the school bus." He loped across the room and grabbed his coat off the hook. "Hey, Pete, can I swap scrubbing the dishes this morning with you and take my turn tonight?"

"Sure, kid."

J.T. yanked open the door and disappeared, the sound of his boots thudding on the porch boards as he hurried toward the barn.

Cade shoved back his chair and stood. "I'd better get going, too. Jed and his brothers will be here soon."

"I'd sure like to hear Mariah laugh more often."

Cade froze, meeting Pete's stern gaze. "Me, too." He walked to the door. "I'll try and make it happen—if she'll give me a chance."

Mariah learned Cade and the Turners were going out to round up the dangerous longhorn cattle at almost the same time Cade was telling Pete and J.T.

This time, Dallas and Grady had lost the toss and had to stay home to run the Turner ranch. The two arrived at the café at their usual time, but without their brothers.

"Hey, you two," Mariah greeted them as they slid into their usual booth. She carried a carafe of coffee and set it on the table in front of them before glancing out the big plate glass window. Only one big truck sat outside. "Where are your brothers?"

"They're over at the Triple C," Grady said glumly.

"Cade and our brothers are heading out this morning to bring in the longhorns," Dallas told her. "Grady and me lost the coin toss so we're stuck taking care of business at home."

Mariah's heart clenched. "Isn't that dangerous?"

"Yeah." Grady's eyes lit. "They're packing pistols and rifles."

"Hey," Dallas said as he laid a hand on Mariah's forearm. "You okay, honey? You're white as a sheet."

"I'm fine," she said faintly, trying to blink away the swift mental image of Cade covered in blood. "Will they have to shoot the longhorns? Are they likely to attack the riders?"

"What? No." Dallas shot a glare at Grady. "Don't tell her they're packing guns without explaining why."

"Hey, I'm sorry." Grady looked genuinely contrite,

his handsome face serious. "Nobody's going to be attacked and it's not likely they'll have to shoot any cattle, either. They took the guns mostly to make noise and drive the cattle. The longhorns are pretty wild so the hope is they'll run from loud noises—in the direction Cade wants them to go."

"Oh, I see." Mariah managed a smile. "I hope it turns out the cattle are better behaved than anyone expects."

Grady and Dallas exchanged a swift glance before turning equally charming smiles on her. "That's probably what will happen," Dallas assured her.

"In the meantime, what can I get you two for breakfast?" Mariah asked in an effort to return to normalcy.

She served their order and made the round of her other customers, chatting and forcing herself to smile until her face hurt. Julie watched her with an occasional worried frown but didn't comment.

When the morning rush ended, however, and the two had time to catch their breath, Julie shoved a coffee cup and a plate holding one of Ed's cinnamon rolls into Mariah's hand.

"Go sit down," she ordered. "Sally, Mariah and I are taking our coffee break," she called into the kitchen.

She barely waited to hear their boss agree before grabbing coffee and a roll of her own and herding Mariah toward the farthest booth, located in the back corner of the café. It was as close to private as they could get.

"All right," Julie said as she slid onto the bench seat across the booth's table from Mariah. "Give, girl. Tell me what's wrong."

"Nothing," Mariah said automatically.

Julie shook her head. "Oh, no you don't. You've been

telling me that ever since the night of the branding party. You're just not yourself. Did Cade do something awful? Because if he did," she said, stabbing the air with her fork for emphasis, "I know at least a dozen guys who will take him out in the alley and beat him up."

The fierce declaration startled a laugh from Mariah.

"There," Julie said with satisfaction. "I haven't heard a real laugh from you in days. Does that mean you want me to find someone to beat up Cade?"

"No!" Mariah shook her head. "I'm a big girl. I can handle my own problems. Besides, Cade didn't do anything that deserves being assaulted."

"Are you sure?" Julie was clearly unconvinced. "Because you seemed so happy with him that night and ever since, you're clearly *not* happy. So of course, I assumed he'd done something to upset you."

"It's not Cade's fault." Mariah toyed with her fork, debating whether to tell Julie. Maybe another woman's opinion would provide a fresh perspective, she decided. She returned the fork to the plate and folded her arms on the tabletop, leaning closer. "I'm upset because Cade thinks I did something underhanded to convince Joseph to give me the cabin at the Triple C. And he doesn't understand that I can't be with a man who believes I'd be so…manipulative," she finished.

Julie's eyes narrowed. "Of course you can't. How can he not understand that?"

Mariah felt a rush of relief at her instant grasp of the situation. "He says he doesn't blame me for wanting a home. And he says it's not personal—every human looks out for number one, even if they don't know they're doing it."

"Boy, is this guy cynical or what?" Julie scoffed. "I'm guessing you told him to get lost until he figures out just how badly he's insulted you? And apologizes?"

"I told him I can't see a future with someone who thinks I'm dishonorable, no matter how great the sex is," she added to herself.

"Whoa, wait a minute." Julie's eyes rounded. "You slept with him?"

"Did I forget to mention that?" Mariah took a big drink of her coffee, wishing she'd not divulged that information.

"And it was amazing, right?"

"Yes," Mariah admitted. "It was more than amazing." She lowered her voice. "I'm in love with him, Julie. And I miss him so much I can hardly stand it. How can I possibly miss him this much after he basically told me he thinks I scammed a very sick man into giving me a valuable piece of property? What does that make me?" She pushed her fingers through her hair and groaned.

"I suspect that makes you a woman in love with a man who's clearly clueless." Julie reached across the table and waggled her hands. "See these?"

Mariah looked but saw nothing out of the ordinary in Julie's slim fingers, neat manicure and rings.

"You have a new manicure?"

"No, no," Julie said impatiently. "The rings."

"I've seen them before—they're nice, really nice. I especially like the blue sapphire."

"The point is, Bob gave me each of them after we had an argument. Both times, he did something so outrageously dumb that he bought me jewelry to apologize."

"I don't understand."

"I'm trying to tell you," Julie said patiently, "that men's brains function differently, on occasion, from women's. What is so obvious to us sometimes is clear as mud to a man. You have to hang in there—if he's a man worthy of you loving him, he'll figure this out and apologize."

"But he truly doesn't seem to get why I was so upset," Mariah told her.

"The important thing here," Julie insisted, "is that he doesn't have to understand why you're upset, he just has to accept that this is important to you. That should be enough for him."

"I like the concept but I'm not sure it will work with Cade. Unlike your husband who had great parents, Cade had a terrible childhood. I'm not sure he's capable of getting past the cynicism."

"I watched him with you at the dance," Julie told her with conviction. "I think he's capable of doing whatever it takes to keep you in his life."

"I hope you're right, Julie." Mariah wished her friend was right, but she wasn't convinced.

Her shift ended at 1:00 p.m. and when she arrived home that afternoon, Cade's pickup wasn't parked outside the house or barn and the horse trailer was missing. Jiggs was gone, too, the corral empty.

Without Cade, the energy seemed gone, she thought as she walked back down the lane a half hour later after showering and changing into boots and jeans. The ranch felt as if it were waiting for him to return, just as it had before he'd arrived weeks ago.

And she missed him.

Despite working double shifts and coming home to clean the house from top to bottom or ride Zelda until she was exhausted, she still dreamed about him when she fell asleep.

And she missed him so much that the ache in her chest felt permanent. It was harder than she'd thought it would be to keep from picking up the phone when he called or answering the door when he knocked.

She really hoped Julie was right about Cade caring for her.

"Hey, Mariah."

She looked up, scanning the ranch yard, and found J.T. in the open doorway to the barn. He raised his hand and beckoned when she saw him.

"What's up?" she called as she neared the barn.

"One of the Herefords dropped a late calf," he told her, grinning when her steps quickened and she hurried past him. He followed her. "I thought you might be interested."

She flashed him a smile over her shoulder. "You were right," she said and kept walking, her strides brisk as she moved quickly down the center aisle of the big barn, out the door at the other end and across the lot to the cattle shed.

One end of the shed was penned off into box stalls and it was here she found the new calf, staggering around the straw bedding on gangly legs.

"He seems fine," she murmured, searching the newborn. The little red and white Hereford bleated, butting at his mother's side as he searched for milk.

"I told Cade at breakfast this morning that I was sure you wouldn't mind helping with new calves." Beside her, J.T. leaned his forearms on the top rail of the pen, watching the calf.

"Was he okay with that?" Mariah asked, her voice carefully noncommittal.

"Didn't say he wasn't." J.T. glanced sideways at her. "What's going on with you two?" he asked bluntly. "Why'd you quit the Triple C?"

"Let's just say Cade and I have a difference of opinion about a few things." Mariah was determined not to cause trouble between Cade and her two friends. Her problems with Cade were extremely personal and not connected to their boss-employee relationship.

J.T. looked unconvinced but fortunately for Mariah, he didn't question her further.

She only wished she was still seeing Cade at breakfast. She missed him and the stalemate between them was breaking her heart.

Chapter Eleven

Mariah wasn't home when the dusty riders drove the first of the longhorns into the holding pens at the Triple C the following day. Over the next week, they drove a series of smaller herds of bulls with cows, the number of cattle swelling until the corrals and pens were full.

Although they knew there were more cattle to collect, the Turners packed their gear and headed home, agreeing with Cade to repeat the roundup when the pens were emptied.

Cade showered and shaved off the beard stubble gained over a week but before he fell into bed, he telephoned a local rodeo stock contractor.

The following day when the stock contractor arrived to look at the Brahma/longhorn mixed-breed cattle, Cade was in no better mood than he'd been in for the last week or two. In fact, he'd been cranky as a grizzly bear ever since arguing with Mariah after they'd made love.

He'd barely caught a glimpse of her car's taillights as she'd driven away early that morning.

Something has to give between us, he thought grimly as he strode across the ranch yard to the holding pens with Jim Ahern.

"I was surprised when you called, Cade," Jim said. "I didn't know the Triple C had any Brahma or longhorn stock."

Ahern's comment drew Cade's attention and he forced himself to focus. The thorny problem of Mariah would have to wait.

"It doesn't look like anybody knew," he said. "I thought Dad sold all of them years ago but apparently he left some bulls and cows in the north and east pastures. They've been out there for years, with nobody bothering them because Dad only used the pastures closest to home."

"So they're essentially wild?"

"Pretty much."

The two men reached the holding pens and climbed one of the high fences to look inside. A heavy black bull with sweeping horns and the distinctive shoulder hump of a Brahma snorted when he saw them, lowering his head and swinging it from side to side.

Jim whistled, long and low. "Damn, Cade, that's one mean-looking animal."

"Yeah," Cade agreed with a solemn nod. "He is that." He pointed across the pens, the bulls and cattle inside them visible from their vantage point. "And there are a lot more just like him."

Ahern's eyes lit with anticipation. "I can use them,"

he said with enthusiasm. "And I know a few other contractors who have been looking for new rodeo stock." He looked sideways at Cade. "But you're going to have to shorten those horns. Nobody's going to buy them without you cutting them first."

"We can do that," Cade told him. "How short do you want them?"

Jim measured with his hands. "No longer than this, maybe."

Cade nodded. "All right. You want to walk around and take a closer look at the rest of them—pick out the ones you want?"

"Absolutely."

The two spent the next hour inspecting the bulls and marking the specific animals the contractor chose. When they shook hands and Ahern drove away, Cade called Jed and they agreed to start sawing off and shortening the dangerous horns the next day.

Mariah made it a point to stay away from the Triple C, working at the café, going shopping and to movies with Julie, sharing dinners with Sally and Ed. Nevertheless, the cabin on the ranch was the only home she had, and she knew she couldn't avoid bumping into Cade forever.

She didn't expect their first encounter to be quite so dramatic, however.

Several days after the last group of longhorns arrived at the ranch, Mariah finished her shift at the café and drove home midafternoon. It was too early for J.T. to be out of school and Pete had told her at the café early that morning that he was on his way to Billings. Pete hadn't mentioned what Cade's plans were for the day but even if he were at home, Mariah didn't plan to talk to him.

There were times when she wondered if she was taking the coward's way out by refusing to talk to him, or see him. But she couldn't come up with another plan. There wasn't a future for them and severing ties was essential. Yet their houses were within the same compound of ranch buildings and it was inevitable that they would see each other.

She couldn't imagine how this would work long-term, and had almost accepted that she would have to move away from the cabin she'd grown to love.

Distracted by gloomy thoughts, she rounded the curve in the lane and drove into the ranch yard. Cade stalked toward the porch steps, his shirt slashed open from shoulder to where it tucked into his belt, bright crimson blood smearing the blue cotton.

Mariah slammed on the brakes, her determination to spend a quiet afternoon at home instantly drowned by fear.

She thrust the door open, leaped out of the car and ran.

"Cade, what happened?" She hurried up the steps and pushed the door inward.

"A bull caught me with a horn," he told her, moving past her into the house.

"One of the longhorns." It wasn't a question, her breath seizing with dread.

"Yeah." He strode down the hall and into a bathroom.

Mariah followed, frowning as he ripped his shirt open, the snaps giving way with quick pops. He winced as he tried to shrug out of the shirt and with sudden decision, she caught his forearm.

"Sit down. I'll do that." She lowered the lid on the commode and pushed him to sit. She could feel his gaze on her as she studied the torn shirt. "There's no saving this," she noted, mostly to herself. She rummaged in a drawer in the cabinet next to the sink and found a pair of scissors. With quick efficiency, she cut the shirt free from his wounded side before unsnapping the cuff on the other arm and stripping the shirt away from him. She tossed the pieces of the stained garment into the bathtub behind her and bent to inspect the long jagged tear in the flesh along his ribs.

"I think he just grazed you," she murmured. "But the doctor will know." She half turned. "I'll get you another shirt. My car's right outside and it won't take too long to reach the hospital...."

"No." Cade's hand closed over her forearm, stopping her. "No doctor. Just pour some antiseptic over the cut, slap a bandaid on it, and I'm good."

Mariah felt her eyes widen as she turned back to fully face him. "Cade, that's an ugly wound. You should see a doctor—you probably need stitches." The injury was raw and seeped blood, his chest and abdomen marked with white scars from older damage.

He shook his head, his jaw set. "I'll be fine. I've been hurt worse lots of times."

She was unconvinced but the stubborn angle of his jaw told her it would do no good to argue with him.

The cabinet over the sink held antiseptic, gauze and several rolls of ace bandages.

"This might sting." Mariah poured antiseptic on a gauze pad and wiped smears of blood from the heavy muscle over his ribs. Much to her relief, removing the blood stains made the jagged tear in his flesh seem less horrible. She took a towel from the bar and used it to catch the excess liquid when she poured the antiseptic directly onto the cut.

Cade sucked in his breath but his body didn't flinch, remaining rock steady as she blotted the excess moisture from his skin and laid a wide gauze pad over the wound. Then she unrolled the ace bandage.

In order to secure the gauze, she had to wrap the elastic bandage around his chest. She had to reach around him, each circle of bandage around his torso meant she had to wrap her arms around his bare body. She didn't look up at him, so close that her hair brushed his throat and jaw, sliding against his pecs and abdomen as she leaned in, then back. The scent of clean male sweat mixed with soap filled her nostrils and it was all she could do not to bury her face against his warm skin and breathe him in. When she finally finished and added a metal clasp to the Velcro grip to secure the end of the bandage, she was breathing too fast. The heat in her cheeks told her that her face was flushed.

"Finished," she said, her voice husky. "I still think you should see a doctor."

"I don't need a doctor." He caught her when she would have moved away.

Mariah met his gaze and was riveted by the heat that darkened his eyes to emerald.

"Cade, I don't think…"

"Shhh." He slid his fingers into her hair, the other hand circling her waist to tug her down to sit in his lap. "Don't think."

And his mouth covered hers. Mariah went under, giving in to the wave of sensual desire that swamped her.

One big hand cradled her head, holding her still for his kiss that ravaged her mouth. The other hand left her waist to stroke down her hip and close over her thigh.

Long heated moments passed. When Cade lifted his head, Mariah's arms were wrapped around his neck, her heartbeat pounding beneath her breast where she pressed against his bare chest.

"Mariah," he muttered, his gaze intent, the lines of his face taut with desire. "We need to talk."

Instantly, she realized she'd done what she'd vowed she wouldn't do—she'd given in to the overwhelming physical need that drew her to him like a magnet.

Before she could push away, he lowered his head, brushing his lips over hers. She fought the instant melting of her resolve.

"I miss you, baby," he murmured roughly. "We're good together—come to bed with me."

"No, I can't," she said, feeling the loss of his warmth as she stood, stepping back. "Please, Cade…" She gestured between them, unable to put into words the depth of feelings that swirled between them. "I have to go."

She turned and walked quickly out of the bathroom, out of the house and to her car. Tears blinded her and she dashed them away as she drove the remaining distance to the cabin.

"I will get over this," she told herself fiercely as she entered the cabin. Physical attraction wouldn't resolve the issue of trust that lay between them. She refused to give in to the need to climb into bed and pull the covers up to cry. Instead, she forced herself to begin a storm of housecleaning, doggedly wiping away tears and the headache that echoed the pain in her chest, right above her heart.

Cade drove into the alley behind the feed store, backing up to the loading dock and leaving his truck to enter the store through the rear entrance.

Archie looked up as Cade strode down the aisle toward the counter.

"Hey, Cade, how's everything out at the Triple C?"

"Not bad, Archie." Cade pulled the sheet of paper with Pete's scribbled notes from his back pocket and handed it to him. "Pete told me to give you this—says you can read his writing. I sure as hell hope so, because I can't."

Archie grinned. "It took me a while to learn but I can usually decipher his scratches." He looked over the list, frowned a couple of times before nodding. "We have all this in stock, I think. Are you parked out back?"

"Yeah." Cade followed Archie down an aisle.

"Six of these bags," Archie told him, grabbing one and levering it over his shoulder.

Cade followed suit and trailed the other man down the aisle and out to the loading dock. They dropped their load into the bed of the pickup truck and went back inside.

"I hear Mariah quit the Triple C." Archie picked up another bag, shifted it onto his shoulder and turned, his gaze meeting Cade's with a directness that demanded an answer. "Folks say there's trouble between you two."

"It's personal," Cade said shortly, irritated that the rift between Mariah and him had become common gossip.

"Just thought I'd warn you." Archie turned and headed down the aisle toward the loading dock, a second bag slung over his shoulder. "I'm not sure it's a good idea for you to try and eat lunch at the café. Sally and Julie might refuse to serve you."

"Did they tell you that?" Cade followed with another bag.

"No, I overheard a couple women talking." Archie dropped the feed sack on top of the others in Cade's pickup bed. "They came in to look at garden seed." He grinned at Cade. "They kept talking the whole time they were in here. It's a toss-up as to which is the hottest topic, speculation about you and Mariah or the likelihood that Ken Eaton's wife really did catch him at the motel in Billings with an exotic dancer from Minneapolis."

Cade lifted an eyebrow. "An exotic dancer from Minneapolis?"

"Yep." Archie headed back inside. "Apparently, old Ken has previously unknown depths to him."

"Huh, you don't say?" Cade replied. He hoped Eaton and his wife kept the gossip mill fueled for a while. He didn't really care what people said about him but he didn't want gossip upsetting Mariah.

Oh, hell, he thought. *I don't want her unhappy.*

He had to find a way to make her listen—and then hope to hell she accepted his apology.

Over the next several days, Cade telephoned and left several messages on Mariah's answering machine. Twice, he knew she was at home but didn't pick up.

Finally, he walked down the lane after dinner one evening and knocked on her door.

She didn't answer.

He waited and knocked once more but again, there was no response. He turned, striding down the steps and past her car, going back down the lane to the ranch house.

He went into the house and straight to the cabinet in the office. The half-filled bottle of Jack Daniels whiskey was exactly where his dad had always kept it. He grabbed it, along with a heavy cut crystal glass, and carried bottle and glass back into the living room. He dropped onto the leather sofa and picked up the control for the television, turning to a cable news channel before tossing the remote onto the leather cushion.

Lifting the bottle, he poured the glass half full before setting the whiskey on the low coffee table. He raised the glass, pausing just before he drank.

Dust coated his fingers.

What the hell? Frowning, he assessed the glass but the etched surface was clear.

He looked at the bottle. The imprint of his hand stood out against the dust on the amber surface.

Joseph Coulter had only been dead for a few months. Could that much dust accumulate in so little time?

He frowned, eyes narrowed as he stared at the bottle.

More than one person in Indian Springs had commented that his dad had stopped drinking years before. He hadn't given their claims a lot of credence. Joseph had never been a man to drink in a bar, or drive drunk, or any other public displays of alcoholism. Mostly, he just drank. Period. He started drinking when he rose in the morning and sipped Jack Daniels whiskey all day long until he fell into bed at night.

And as the hours passed, he'd grown meaner.

Cade couldn't count the number of times Joseph's vicious temper had exploded in blows. He didn't want to remember the number of times he'd stepped between his father and one of his younger brothers, taking the punishment for them. The day he'd driven away from the Triple C, he'd put all that behind him.

Was it possible his father really had changed when he and his brothers left? Had he come to regret the years he'd lost to alcohol and despair over the death of his wife?

Had Joseph Coulter actually stopped blaming his sons for their mother's death?

Cade leaned forward, propping his elbows on his knees, the glass dangling between them as memory sucked him in.

The sun had been shining, the sky as bright as the bluebells his mother had loved, on the day she died. She'd laughed at her sons from the porch of her studio, teasing them to swing higher, farther, on the rope that dangled from the old tree overhanging the deep pool in the creek.

They all complied, striving to make her shriek louder as they pushed the limits of their young bodies. Zach landed with a huge splash and came up sputtering, crowing with delight. He taunted their mother, challenging her to beat his record and she'd left the porch, running down the creek bank to join them.

"Melanie, no!" Joseph's roar reached her but it was too late. She was already launching herself, clutching the rope in both hands, her shorts and top splashed with water from the boys below. Then the rope broke. And she fell.

Cade had never forgotten the sound of her head hitting the rock on the creek bank.

Two days later, Melanie Coulter, beloved wife and mother, was dead from brain trauma.

Grief stricken, Joseph Coulter blamed his sons. His drinking plunged them all into a hell that only ended for his sons when they left the Triple C, all four of them together, when Eli graduated from high school.

Cade shook his head, the sound of the cable news announcer yanking him out of the past and back to the present. He lifted the glass and tossed back the whiskey, feeling the burn as it slid down his throat.

And his chest burned, too. The odd numbness that had gripped his emotions since he'd returned to the Triple C was gone, replaced by a storm of emotion.

He stared at the glass, rolling it between his palms.

He rarely drank alcohol. He wasn't a teetotaler but growing up with an alcoholic had made him wary of the stuff.

Face it, Coulter, he thought. *If you don't fix this trouble with Mariah, you might turn out just like your dad.*

For the first time in his life, Cade had a flash of understanding for his father. And he knew, without a shadow of a doubt, that he would never do what Joseph Coulter had done. The lessons he'd learned as a boy when his mother died had cut too deep.

If he was lucky enough to have children with the woman he loved, he would never abandon them to lose himself in grief.

And Mariah was the woman he loved—every bit as much as his father had loved his mother.

The question was— How in hell was he going to convince her?

* * *

The café wasn't quite half-full at ten o'clock. Regular customers on their morning coffee break sat at tables, in booths, or perched on the blue vinyl stools at the counter.

Mariah had been busy since five o'clock and was glad to be working behind the counter.

The bells hung on the front door jingled and she glanced up.

Cade stepped into the café, the plate glass door closing behind him as his gaze swept the room.

Mariah met his eyes with equanimity before looking away. She'd known it was only a matter of time before he sought her out here. After all, it was the one place he would be sure she couldn't avoid him.

He strode across the room, stopping in front of the counter.

"Mariah, will you step outside with me for a minute?"

"I'm sorry, I can't, Cade. I'm working."

"I'd rather talk to you without an audience."

"I'm sorry, Cade," she repeated, murmuring in an effort to keep the interested customers from hearing.

He studied her, his voice at normal level when he spoke. "Mariah Jones, I want you to come back to work on the Triple C."

"No, thank you," she said politely, thinking he clearly didn't care if the entire café heard their conversation.

"Why not?"

"You know why not. We discussed this. And nothing has changed."

"Everything's changed."

"How? What's different?"

"I've realized I was wrong."

Her heart stopped, then sped up, beating faster than before. "In what way?" she asked carefully, hardly daring to hope.

"You couldn't have conned Joseph into leaving you the cabin."

"Why not?"

"Because you're honest. Sometimes," he amended as his mouth curved in a brief, rueful grin, "you're *too* honest."

"Thank you for telling me," she said gravely. "It means a lot."

"So." He lifted an eyebrow. "You'll be working at the Triple C again?"

"No."

His brows drew down. "Why not?"

"I don't think it's wise."

He stared at her for a long moment. "Can we please have a word in private?"

She shook her head. "I don't think that's wise, either." She knew very well that if they were alone, her weakened resolve would have her in his arms within seconds.

His green eyes narrowed with intent while he studied her for a long moment.

"If we can't do this in private, then we'll do it in public," he said at last, his deep voice an amused drawl.

"Do what?" she asked, bemused.

He moved forward until only the counter separated them, his gaze holding hers.

Every customer in the place turned to watch them. Sally and Julie stopped clearing tables to observe and even Ed peered through the pass-through from the kitchen.

"Mariah Jones." His deep voice carried clearly throughout the quiet room, reaching every ear. "Will you marry me?"

Staggered, she stared at him in shock. "What?" she managed to whisper into the expectant silence.

"I asked you to marry me. I'm crazy about you." He leaned over the counter until their noses nearly touched. "Come back to the Triple C. Let's get married, have babies, all that settled-down stuff that people in love do."

When she didn't answer and only stared at him with wide eyes, his brows lowered. "Unless you don't want to?"

Her eyes widened farther and a smile trembled on her lips. "Oh, I do," she said fervently. "I really do."

And she launched herself at him. His big hands closed around her waist and he lifted her up and over the counter. His mouth took hers at the same time as his arms wrapped her tightly against him.

Around them, the café broke into cheers and shrieks of delight but Mariah barely heard them. Happiness fizzed and zinged through her veins.

At last, his mouth released hers and he lifted his head just far enough to look into her eyes.

"Are you ready to go home?" His green eyes glowed with heat and a smile curved his mouth.

"Oh, yes," she murmured, smiling up at him.

He bent and slipped an arm under her knees, swinging her up in his arms.

The customers burst into whoops and whistles as

Cade carried Mariah out of the café and she buried her face against the warm column of his throat.

"I love you," she breathed against his skin.

"I love you, too." He paused to press a brief, hard kiss against her lips.

Mariah wrapped her arms around his neck and held him close, dizzied by the speed with which the future had gone from dismal to a horizon of infinite possibility, filled with love, happiness and best of all, Cade.

Epilogue

"Hey, honey," Cade's voice called. "Where are you?"

"I'm in the kitchen," she called back. Drying her hands on a tea towel, Mariah walked toward the living room but barely made it past the breakfast nook when Cade entered the kitchen.

"Pete went to town. He said to tell you if you think of anything you need, you can reach him at the café in an hour."

Cade brought with him the scent of sage, fresh air and leather. Mariah's heart caught as he grinned at her, just before he swept her from head to toe with a glance that turned his green eyes hot.

He strode across the tiled floor and caught her around the waist, lifting her on tiptoe to take her mouth in a kiss that sizzled along her nerve endings. When he lifted his head and let her lower her heels to the floor, she was aroused and hungry.

"What was that for?" she got out, her fingers threaded into the thick black hair at his nape.

"Nothing. You're just so damned pretty that I can't be around you without kissing you." He stroked the tip of his forefinger over the lush curve of her lower lip. "Or tasting you."

He lowered his head and took her mouth again. When he lifted his head at last, his eyes were heavy lidded with arousal, one hand cupping her breast beneath her shirt. His thumb brushed back and forth over her beaded nipple covered by the soft lace of her bra and she caught her breath, pressing against his hand.

He walked her backward and with one easy movement, picked her up and set her on the kitchen counter. He nudged her knees apart and stepped between them, snugging his arousal into the vee of her thighs.

Mariah gasped and dragged his mouth back down to hers.

For long moments, the charged air in the kitchen grew hotter, breathing coming faster, more ragged.

Just when Mariah knew she could bear no more teasing, a telephone rang. Both she and Cade ignored it. The rings continued.

"Do you need to answer that?" Cade's voice rasped, roughened with arousal.

"No. Wait…." She suddenly realized the ring tone wasn't hers. "It's not my phone."

Cade growled out a curse and yanked his cell phone from his shirt pocket. Without releasing Mariah, he flipped open the phone and thumbed the on switch. "Yeah."

The hard body pressed to Mariah's went still, taut with surprise, and Cade's green eyes sharpened, losing the fog of arousal.

"Where the hell have you been, Zach?" He waited, listening. "Good to know you survived," he commented. "There's no easy way to say this, Zach. The old man died. He left the Triple C to you, me, Eli and Brodie. I'm in Indian Springs and I need you to come home."

Cade's free hand moved, his fingers stroking slow, testing circles against the bare skin of her back just below the waistband of her jeans.

Mariah shivered, her hands tightening in his hair. His lashes lifted, green gaze pinning hers as he listened to his brother on the other end of the phone.

"I left a message on Eli's machine to call me but I haven't heard from him." Cade frowned. "And I have no idea where the hell Brodie is—the last phone number I had for him isn't any good anymore. Have you heard from him over the last six to eight months?" His frown deepened as he clearly listened to Zach's response. "Damn. I was hoping you'd talked to him." He fell silent, nodding at last. "All right. Let me know if you need a ride from the airport. And Zach…" He paused. "I'm glad you're coming home." Another pause. "Right. See you soon."

He hit the off switch and tossed the phone on the counter.

"Where were we?" He slipped his hand beneath the hem of Mariah's shirt and cupped the weight of her breast in his hand. "Oh, yeah," he murmured. "Right about here…."

Mariah caught his hand, holding him still. "Wait.

Tell me—that was your brother, right? He's coming to help?"

"Yes, that was Zach. And yes, he's coming home."

"Soon?" she pushed, hoping.

"Yeah, soon. Or as soon as it's possible to get here from Nepal," Cade added. "I have no idea how long that takes."

"I don't know, either, but I'm so glad he's on his way." Mariah smiled up at him, relieved. "I was beginning to worry about how long it would take to find your brothers."

"I told you not to worry, honey. We stay in touch."

"Only guys would consider once a year or so 'keeping in touch,'" she told him.

Cade shrugged. "I'm more interested in you and me keeping in touch," he told her, his voice deepening. "Now, where were we...."

Mariah took her hand from his, relishing the instant movement of his fingers on the sensitive skin of her breast.

"I think we were..." she wrapped her arms around his neck and slipped her fingers into the silky hair at his nape once more "...right here."

His lips curved in a sensual half smile, his green eyes instantly heavy lidded as he lowered his mouth to hers.

Awash in sensation, Mariah realized with hazy delight that Cade had brought her all the love, intimacy and happiness she'd ever dreamed of. He was her family, she thought just before she stopped thinking and gave in to a tidal wave of passion.

* * * * *

Look for Zach Coulter's story,
THE VIRGIN AND ZACH COULTER.
Coming to Silhouette Special Edition.

SPECIAL EDITION

COMING NEXT MONTH

Available October 26, 2010

#2077 EXPECTING THE BOSS'S BABY
Christine Rimmer
Bravo Family Ties

#2078 ONCE UPON A PROPOSAL
Allison Leigh
The Hunt for Cinderella

#2079 THUNDER CANYON HOMECOMING
Brenda Harlen
Montana Mavericks: Thunder Canyon Cowboys

#2080 UNDER THE MISTLETOE WITH JOHN DOE
Judy Duarte
Brighton Valley Medical Center

#2081 THE BILLIONAIRE'S HANDLER
Jennifer Greene

#2082 ACCIDENTAL HEIRESS
Nancy Robards Thompson

REQUEST YOUR FREE BOOKS!

2 FREE NOVELS PLUS 2 FREE GIFTS!

SPECIAL EDITION
Life, Love and Family!

YES! Please send me 2 FREE Silhouette® Special Edition® novels and my 2 FREE gifts (gifts are worth about $10). After receiving them, if I don't wish to receive any more books, I can return the shipping statement marked "cancel." If I don't cancel, I will receive 6 brand-new novels every month and be billed just $4.24 per book in the U.S. or $4.99 per book in Canada. That's a saving of 15% off the cover price! It's quite a bargain! Shipping and handling is just 50¢ per book.* I understand that accepting the 2 free books and gifts places me under no obligation to buy anything. I can always return a shipment and cancel at any time. Even if I never buy another book from Silhouette, the two free books and gifts are mine to keep forever.

235/335 SDN E5RG

Name	(PLEASE PRINT)

Address	Apt. #

City	State/Prov.	Zip/Postal Code

Signature (if under 18, a parent or guardian must sign)

Mail to the Silhouette Reader Service:
IN U.S.A.: P.O. Box 1867, Buffalo, NY 14240-1867
IN CANADA: P.O. Box 609, Fort Erie, Ontario L2A 5X3

Not valid for current subscribers to Silhouette Special Edition books.

Want to try two free books from another line?
Call 1-800-873-8635 or visit www.morefreebooks.com.

* Terms and prices subject to change without notice. Prices do not include applicable taxes. N.Y. residents add applicable sales tax. Canadian residents will be charged applicable provincial taxes and GST. Offer not valid in Quebec. This offer is limited to one order per household. All orders subject to approval. Credit or debit balances in a customer's account(s) may be offset by any other outstanding balance owed by or to the customer. Please allow 4 to 6 weeks for delivery. Offer available while quantities last.

Your Privacy: Silhouette is committed to protecting your privacy. Our Privacy Policy is available online at www.eHarlequin.com or upon request from the Reader Service. From time to time we make our lists of customers available to reputable third parties who may have a product or service of interest to you. If you would prefer we not share your name and address, please check here. ☐

Help us get it right—We strive for accurate, respectful and relevant communications. To clarify or modify your communication preferences, visit us at www.ReaderService.com/consumerchoice.

SSE10R

Spotlight on
Inspirational

Wholesome romances
that touch the heart and soul.

See the next page
to enjoy a sneak peek from
the Love Inspired® Suspense
inspirational series.

*See below for a sneak peek from
our inspirational line, Love Inspired® Suspense*

*Enjoy this heart-stopping excerpt from
RUNNING BLIND
by top author Shirlee McCoy,
available November 2010!*

**The mission trip to Mexico was supposed to be an
adventure. But the thrill turns sour when Jenna Dougherty
and her roommate Magdalena are kidnapped.**

"It's okay. I'm here to help." The voice was as deep as the
darkness, but Jenna Dougherty didn't believe the lie. She
could do nothing but lie still as hands slid down her arms,
felt the rope around her wrists.

"I'm going to use a knife to cut you free, Jenna. Hold
still."

The cold blade of a knife pressed close to her head before
her gag fell away.

"I—" she started, but her mouth was dry, and she could
do nothing but suck in air.

"Shhh. Whatever needs to be said can be said when
we're out of here." Nick spoke quietly, his hand gentle on
her cheek. There and gone as he sliced through the ropes on
her wrists and ankles.

He pulled her upright. "Come on. We may be on
borrowed time."

"I can't leave my friend," Jenna rasped out.

"There's no one here. Just us."

"She has to be here." Jenna took a step away.

"There's no one here. Let's go before that changes."

"It's dark. Maybe if we find a light…"

"What did you say?"

SHLISEXP1110

"We need to turn on the light. I can't leave until I know that—"

"What can you see, Jenna?"

"Nothing."

"No shadows? No light?"

"No."

"It's broad daylight. There's light spilling in from the window I climbed in through. You can't see it?"

She went cold at his words.

"I can't see anything."

"You've got a nasty bruise on your forehead. Maybe that has something to do with it." His fingers traced the tender flesh on her forehead.

"It doesn't matter *how* it happened. I'm blind!"

Can Nick help Jenna find her friend or will chasing this trail have Jenna running blindly again into danger?

Find out in RUNNING BLIND, available in November 2010 only from Love Inspired Suspense.

SHLISEXP1110